Mystical
Mortality

Diana Marie DuBois

Mystical Mortality

Diana Marie DuBois

Published by Three Danes Publishing L.L.C.

Cover art by Anya Kelleye
http://www.anyakelleye.com/
Photographer Stacey Powell
Model Victor Arroyo III
Edited by Maxine Horton Bringenberg and Beth Lake

My Acknowledgements

~Jessi Gibson, the best author coach I could ask for. Thanks for all of your encouragement. I couldn't have done this without you.

~Stacey Powell, oh my gawd where do I start. Thanks for joining me on this wild and crazy adventure to New Orleans in the great flood, to shoot for the cover. From the black cat crossing your path to people recognizing Victor at the cemetery and all the laughs we had with him. You sure know how to keep a secret.

~Anya damn girl you are a whiz at making covers. This is my fave so far.

~Anita, for keeping a secret and just being there for me.

~My editors and proofreader who polish my stories for me. I love ya'll.

~To all my fans, I hope you enjoy this story as much as I did writing it.

~Lastly, Victor thanks for agreeing to grace my cover and becoming Maxim Rafferty.

Dedication

Victor, for just being you. I hope I've done you proud. I swear as I wrote this story your laugh resonated in my head.

Note to Readers

I must confess I faithfully watch only one reality TV show. I've watched it from the very beginning. That being said when I watched it in 2016, one participant caught my eye. At that moment I wanted him on a cover. It took a year for me to get in touch with him, but when I did my dreams came true. Victor agreed to a photoshoot. This story was his idea with my paranormal twist on it, told from within the house. It's also a love story of a forbidden love. I invite you to enter the Mystical Mansion, at your own risk of course. If you do decide to enter, I promise you one hell of an adventure.

Be careful what you wish for. There's always a catch.

~Laurie Halse Anderson

Prologue

As my car careened down the interstate, one of the many arguments I had with my father played on a continuous loop like a film reel in my head.

"Damn it, Maxim, don't you want to be alpha?"
I shook my head. "No, Dad. I don't."
He slammed his fist on the table. "The council will not appreciate this."
"I don't care," I replied.
"Don't you care about someone else taking over my throne?"
I thought for a slight second, and then my shoulders slumped. I couldn't answer him, so I walked away. Sadness wrapped around me as I knew I'd disappointed my father, but I wanted my own life, not his.

I thrummed my fingers on the leather steering wheel and quickly passed an eighteen-wheeler. The piece of paper lying beside me on the bench seat caught my eye. I scooped it up and pressed it against the wheel. *Damn, if my father had any inkling of what I was up to he'd probably never forgive me.* I shrugged as I crossed the Tchfuncte River, and remembered where I'd seen the flyer.

Talking to my mother, I'd hoped she'd see my side of the ongoing conflict between my father and me. But as much as she tried to see what I was going through, she still tried to persuade me to take my father's place. So I left and went for a run. It always cleared my head. As my feet pounded on the pavement, I ran across my family's land. When I crossed over the small bridge connecting my father's land to the rest of the pack, I saw something floating in the air. I sucked in a deep breath and stopped. The air blew around me, and a chill crawled up my spine. I breathed in and bent over, catching my breath. Closing my eyes, I let the air swirl around me and sensed I wasn't alone. My ears perked at the sound of paper crinkling, and I swung my head around looking for the cause of the noise. I saw nothing but a piece of paper floating softly to the ground settling near my feet. Without hesitating, I picked it up.

"This may be what you are searching for," a *voice floated on the wind.*

"What? Who said that?" When I glanced around no one was there.

I smoothed out the flyer and read the words. "Holy shit, what in the world?" The sound of feet crunching in the grass caused me to turn, but when I did, I saw nothing.

"Shit!" In front of me a car skidded to a stop, causing me to slam on my brakes and steer my car onto the shoulder before I rear-ended them. My car's tires squealed as I jammed the brakes into the floorboard. The smell of burnt rubber sifted around me, and I coughed loudly. All the vehicles kept going around me, blowing their horns and flipping me off.

"Fuck, this wasn't my fault," I screamed to no one. After a few seconds, I pulled the car back onto the interstate and continued.

Only about another hour and my destiny would be sealed.

One

Before me stood the huge iron gates leading to my redemption. I'd joined the reality show to rid myself of this wretched curse. Without hesitation I placed my hand on the cold iron and pushed the gates open, wincing at their creak as I stepped inside.

Up ahead a crowd of people was gathered around a tomb. As I stepped forward, a black cat skittered under my feet, almost causing me to fall. "Hey, get out of here, mangy cat," I growled. It stopped and glanced in my direction, but quickly darted off.

When I got closer to the crowd, I saw a skeletal man dressed in finery, leaning against the tomb with an eerie smile on his face. Atop his head sat a black top hat lined with feathers and tiny skulls. A huge yellow snake draped itself over his shoulders. My attention turned to a camera poised right above the tomb. Out of the corner of my eye, I noticed a dozen or so more placed in inconspicuous locations.

"All candidates please come forward," the skeletal man hissed and waved us forward.

I inched through the crowd to claim my spot. My nerves rattled throughout my body but stopped short when I saw her. Her long blonde hair fell past her shoulders as the round-rimmed glasses framed her face. Her silvery wings flapped once or twice in sync with my heart. A soft light glowed all around her as if she was inside a bubble of light.

I shook my head in disbelief. She was the most beautiful creature I'd ever seen. "She will be the end of me," I mumbled under my breath. She smiled as she caught me staring at her. The expression mesmerized me and held me prisoner in my spot. Without notice the sky lit up with lightning, followed by a crack of thunder.

Besides the fairy and me, there were fourteen other paranormal creatures. A slight tug on my pant leg caused me to down. A little gnome glared up at me, stroking his beard. "You're blocking my view, wolf."

Laughing nervously, I backed away a little since the rumors of gnomes was well known. "I'm sorry, man."

"No harm," he said, jumping up and standing on my shoulder. His boots dug into me.

On further inspection of the little miscreant, I saw a shiny gold hoop in his nose. He wore a leather jacket, which I found odd since we were in south Louisiana and it wasn't your everyday garden gnome attire...well, except for the hat. He reminded me of a small punk rocker, though gnomes were smarter than the average creature. I wanted to swat him off but thought better of it. I didn't really want to start having any enemies in the house.

We stood in our spots as the sky darkened and night fell, causing the shadows to disappear into the ground. I glanced into the sky, hoping we would hurry and enter the house before the rain drenched us. As the thoughts exited my mind, our host spoke loudly.

"Ladies and gents," the skeletal man spoke. He tapped his staff, laden with a dozen tiny skeleton heads, on the cement floor of the tomb. The heads clacked against each other as he hit it on the floor. He removed his hat and elaborately bowed to the crowd, then waited for the inevitable hush to fall over the onlookers. He placed his hat back on his alabaster head. "I'm your host, Baron Samedi." He pointed to the crowd with his staff, then turned it on the fifteen of us. "Never has anyone in the Big Easy witnessed what you are about to." He waved his bony hand toward the creaking mausoleum door. "These doors lead to a maze of catacombs. Once inside you will not be able to leave until your time is up. Sixteen will enter, but only one will come out. Whoever wins will be granted the gift of mortality. The way into the house is through the tunnels. If you take the wrong one, you will forever be trapped underground. So, without further ado...." He inhaled his cigar and let out the smoke, which danced around shaped like a dozen skeletons.

I glanced around and looked at the others, then my focus went straight back to her. Her pearlescent wings flapped in the nonexistent wind. Trying to pry my eyes from her beauty, I focused on the others.

"You will never have her." The little gnome grinned and jumped off my shoulder. He pushed his way past the others to be first through the tunnels. The others grumbled loudly at his persistence, but he ignored them. I shook my head and returned my attention to Baron Samedi.

He opened the door, and it creaked and scraped against the cement. "You may now enter the Mystical Mansion." He paused, then let out a creepy laugh. "That is, if you dare."

One by one, we entered. Some took different paths, but a little ways ahead the fairy floated, searching one tunnel, then another. I stepped forward, wanting to help her, but something rubbed against my leg, stopping me. I glanced down and saw the black cat nudging my leg. Without thinking, I let out a loud growl. The cat hissed and swatted at me, then stalked off, swishing its tail from side to side.

Don't growl at me, wolf boy. The sound bounced off the inside of my head.

I shook my head, dislodging the noise. "What the hell? Who said that? Am I crazy?"

You're not crazy. I'm talking in your head.

I glanced at the cat who sat licking one paw, then the other. "How's this possible?" I asked in disbelief.

Don't ask questions. Now, would you like to find your way to the house?

"You know which way it is?" I asked in shock, wondering how in the hell a cat would know the way.

The feline licked its paw and cocked her head at me. *Yes, my fine hairy friend. I'm a fountain of secrets. I know all here in the city of the dead. Now follow me.*

I did as it instructed and looked for the fairy, who had vanished. "Damn you cat, you made me miss her."

Please, she's so out of your league.

"Why the hell does everyone keep telling me that?"

That cat never answered me, just continued through a tunnel.

As we passed tunnel after tunnel, I thought maybe the cat was leading me to certain death. Off in the distance, I saw an old cemetery. I stopped and watched an old groundskeeper dust off the tombs. On closer inspection, I noticed none had names on them. My head swam as if I had entered some sort of an alternate reality. "What is that?" I asked the cat as she plodded down the path.

She turned and glanced around. *I see nothing.*

"What do you mean? It's right there...an old cemetery." I turned around and it had disappeared. "Damn, it was just there." I removed my glasses, cleaned them off, and shoved them back on my face as if them being dirty was the reason the cemetery had suddenly disappeared. In fact, I didn't really need the glasses; they just made me appear more human. Without them people noticed me more, and I was trying to blend in.

Hurry up. We are close to the house. The cat ran ahead, swishing her tail back and forth.

I shook my head and took one more glance, but where the tombs had been nothing remained but a few old cypress trees, their moss dancing in the nonexistent breeze.

Down the next pathway, I tripped over something on the ground. "Shit!" I exclaimed and braced my hands to help myself stand. As I pushed myself against the slimy wall, I stared into the face of a dingy yellow skull. The stench of decay took over, and all I smelled was death. Halfway up I grabbed the wall, but my hand slid down the slickness. Pulling my hand back, I grimaced as I saw that black sludge coated it. "What is this?" I asked out loud.

Do you really want to know?

I sniffed my hand and grimaced. "Not really."

Then don't worry about it. We're almost there, the cat said. Finally, after the last turn there before me stood a dingy door.

"Is that it?"

The cat nudged me, pressing against me, then reached up, and dragged its claws to the end of my pants leg.

"Ow," I growled.

It hissed. *Hurry up, your fairy is inside.* The cat grinned.

"How do you know?"

Again, I know all. Now get inside. I'll be around to check on you. Nonetheless if you need me sooner, call out the name Zora and I'll come.

I shook my head. *This is crazy,* I thought to myself. Zora stalked after a mouse that crossed her path as I turned the knob on the door, which creaked open to reveal an extravagant house.

Standing in the doorway like a bright shining light was the fairy. Her hair was different, pulled into a beautiful messy bun atop her head. Her glasses sat on the tip of her nose and she glared at me. She pushed them up and fluttered off.

"Damn, I have a job ahead of me to win her over," I muttered to myself.

When she left, I saw a huge black marble fireplace. Candles lined the mantel and small flames burned inside. I noticed the chill in the air. I was surprised by the fireplace since in New Orleans it rarely got cold enough for such things. But being an old house and probably having no central air and heat, maybe there was a need for it.

Over to the right, sprawled on the black sofa, sat the gnome. His short little legs were pulled close to his chest at the knees, and on his feet were mismatched socks and biker boots. He spoke without looking at me. "It's about time you arrived." He grimaced and stroked his black beard.

I grinned nervously. "Yeah, I took a couple of wrong turns and had to double back," I lied, sitting beside him.

I noticed on his hat the initials FS. I went to ask him what they stood for, but he nudged me. "Don't get involved with the fairy; your job is to win."

"Wait, what about you?"

He sneered. "Oh, I'm just here for the fun. I really don't want to be human. I rather enjoy being a gnome." He sat and leaned forward. "I want to cause a ruckus in the house, among other things." I had a feeling the gnome would be an alliance in the house. It was possible he could be my ride or die. Yet I still had to see if he was actually trustworthy.

The others sat back, chatting and waiting for more to come. I toured the house and noticed cameras in places, just like at the entrance to the tomb. The massive house contained all the amenities to keep all of us comfortable. I glanced around and even saw a chess table. On further inspection I noticed pieces moved by themselves. I blinked and they stopped, but as if an invisible force played, they moved again.

I turned around and saw the fairy staring in my direction. When I caught her, she blushed and dropped her head. One of the others grabbed her by the hand and glared at me, then whisked her away.

I focused my attention on the rest of the house as a clock ticked loudly. Looking around, I noticed a huge, elaborate gothic clock on the wall. As the skeletal hands ticked, we realized no one else was coming.

In a flash Baron Samedi appeared, a cigar stuck firmly in his mouth as he spoke. "Well folks, it seems you are the only ones that have made it to the house."

He removed the cigar and blew black smoke all around us. The fog shaped skeletons danced around us, reaching out their hazy skeletal arms as they wafted around us. He stuck the stogie back in his mouth and looked around, counting. As I watched, I wondered how it stayed there, since his mouth was devoid of some teeth.

He walked through the house, black staff in hand. The skulls moved with his movements, almost grinning at us. He twirled around and faced us. "So, there are less than half of you left to compete. Half of the original members."

"Where are they?" I asked.

The skeletal man glared at me. "Not something you need to worry about."

"Why?" I asked.

"Because soon all of you will be gone but one." He laughed maniacally. "Let the games begin tomorrow morning. Tonight, get to know each other, and after, let the backstabbing begin." His laugh echoed off the walls after he had disappeared.

We all settled in the living room, and someone passed around glasses of champagne. We went around the room introducing ourselves. "Hi, I'm Corbin, I'm a goblin."

A pretty brunette spoke next. "My name is Sally, and I'm a selkie."

My turn was next and I looked around, searching for the fairy, but she was nestled next to the guy who had grabbed her hand earlier. I sniffed the air and smelled something ancient. *Holy shit, he's a dragon,* I thought to myself.

Maybe they are together. But I couldn't help remembering the way she'd watched me before. So I shook off those thoughts and stood. "My name is Maxim, and I am a werewolf." I saw the selkie glance at me, but I only had eyes for the fairy. The gnome nudged me. His glare reminded me that I needed to concentrate on the end...to be human.

The gnome jumped up and grinned, then tipped his red hat. "I'm Saul," he said as he twirled his mustache.

Next was the dragon, whose wings were spread out wide. "I'm Griff." He glared in my direction.

But I couldn't pay attention to him because the fairy was next. Her voice was music to my ears. "Hi everyone, my name is Mariwen."

The last of the creatures to speak was a beautiful ebony woman who stood glass in hand, and brushed back her long hair, revealing pointy ears. "I'm Vanity, and I am an elf."

After all the introductions, exhaustion overtook my senses. The others meandered around the house searching for something to do, but all I wanted was to sleep. I crawled up the steps to the bedrooms. My hands slid along the banister, and the sensation that my hands were touching a snake was confirmed when the head of a snake hissed at me at the top of the macabre staircase. I sensed Saul following me but ignored him.

I found the door with my name on it and opened it to see the room was lit by pale candles, causing shadows to dance on the black painted walls. I slumped down on the crimson-covered bed. As soon as my head hit the pillow, I fell asleep.

TWO

I woke to a creepy sensation of someone watching me. Blinking open my eyes, I scanned the room for anything. Suddenly an apparition appeared before my face, inches from my nose. "What the hell?" I screamed, as panic momentarily bubbled in my chest.

The little girl waved furiously at me, then sat back on the bed with her legs pulled close to her. She wore an ankle length dress. "Hello. Were you sleeping?" she asked in a high-pitched squeal.

"Shh, you'll wake the others."

She shook her head. "Nuh uh. I've already tried. The mean gnome swatted me away from him."

I followed her gaze and saw Saul curled up in the chair in my room. His red hat covered his face, and his leather jacket was draped over him. From under the jacket, a pair of mismatched socks came into view. His boots were haphazardly placed on the floor. I wondered when he had snuck in.

I laughed lightly. "Why are you trying to wake people up?" I questioned her.

"Because I'm bored," she whined in a sing-song voice. She cocked her head at me. "What's your name?"

"Maxim." I yawned.

She squeaked out. "My name is Eloise, and I'm dead."

I rubbed my eyes, sighed and shoved my glasses on my face. "How did you die?"

"That's a long story. Maybe I'll tell you some other time." She smiled.

Sitting, I rubbed my chin, realizing I'd shifted some time during the night. "What in the world?"

She giggled. "You are all hairy."

"I know, but how? It's not a full moon yet."

"The house is magical. It causes those of you that can shift to do so even when it's not time." She giggled again, covering her mouth.

Before I could stop him, Saul stomped over to us. He hopped onto the bed and eyed us both, but returned his gaze to me. "Look, wolf boy, I'm trying to get some shut-eye. We've got a big competition tomorrow. Tell your little ghost friend to beat it." He stuck out his tongue at the ghost as he dug something out of his beard and ate it.

"Yucky. Mr. Meanie." She groaned in protest and disappeared in a flash.

I growled and rolled back over in bed. Saul sat on the edge of my bed peering over at me. "What do you want?" I growled in frustration and exhaustion.

"To have an alliance with you."

"With me?" I asked with curiosity. "Why me?" I was leery of his fascination with me.

"Because out of all these other yahoos here I think you and I can take this house and win." He jumped off the bed with a small thud.

I shook my head and watched him walk away. That was when I saw it...the gnome had a huge tattoo on his back. In the darkness, I couldn't make it out, but maybe tomorrow. Tonight, I was exhausted.

The next morning

As I woke, this time by myself and not with the help of some ghost kid, I looked around my room. Quickly I jumped out of bed and glanced in the mirror. Thank goodness I had returned to normal. "Damn, it will be nice to be rid of this curse once and for all," I muttered to myself.

As I entered the cold marble and glass shower, against my better judgment I contemplated seeing the fairy this morning. After my shower, I dried and shoved my legs into a pair of jeans, threw a T-shirt over my head, and tied my wet hair into a bun.

I stalked outside and downstairs. My bare feet slapped against the marble floor of the hallway. I entered the kitchen, and the scent of maple syrup wafted over to me. I peered around the corner and noticed Saul standing on the counter, spatula in hand. He flipped pancakes in the air, letting them land in the skillet with precision I'd never seen coming from a creature of his stature. I grinned wide.

"Where is everyone?" I pulled a chair out and sat, leaning on my elbows.

"Still asleep. Which gives us a chance to talk game." He tossed a pancake onto a plate and pointed at it. "What, you want me to bring it over to you too?" he grimaced.

"No, I can get it." I scooted my chair out and walked over to the stove where my plate waited for me. The smell of butter and syrup permeated my nostrils, causing my stomach to growl. "Sorry," I laughed.

"No problem. I did sort of peg you for the raw meat kind of guy." He cocked his head and grinned, causing his hat to topple off to the floor. He waved his hand and it flew back into place before I could comment on his Mohawk. I chuckled, grabbed a fork and knife, and went back to the table. The moment the pancake hit my tongue I sighed. "Damn, Saul, this is delicious."

"What's delicious?" The singsongy voice made my head spin.

"Mariwen?" I choked out her name as a piece of food got stuck in my throat.

She rolled her eyes at me and floated over to Saul. "Ooh, that smells divine," she cooed.

"Don't try to be flattering me, wing girl." He tossed a pancake on a plate for her and secretly smiled. I grinned at the thought he wasn't such a hardass after all. Though I sure to hell wouldn't ever tell him that observation.

A while later the others trickled downstairs. A loud voice boomed through the house. "Please assemble in the dining room for breakfast."

"Damn, if I'd know they were serving food I wouldn't have cooked."

"Saul, I'd prefer pancakes any day." Mariwen laughed and took her plate into the other room.

"See, you have a fan, Saul." I chuckled loudly, grabbed my plate, and followed him.

We joined the others for a bite to eat, which appeared before us as we sat...any kind of breakfast food we could imagine. I stared at my plate to see a raw steak. I pushed the steak away and continued to eat the pancakes Saul had made. Saul was daintily eating his plants. I barely glanced at the others and ate my own breakfast. I kept an eye on Mari, who kept close contact with the smarmy dragon. I wanted to scream to her he wasn't good for her.

"Stop it, Max." Saul leaned on my leg. "You need to get your mind on the game or you may lose." He sauntered off, still talking. "I kind of would hate to see you go." He turned and faced me, his eyes dark. "But if you ever repeat that I'll kill you in your sleep."

My eyes grew wide with fake shock, and I crossed my hands over my chest. "I swear on my mother's soul, may it rest in hell." I laughed out as he waved my sarcasm off.

Once we'd all had our fill, Baron popped in with a glass of rum in his hand. In the other, he held a cigar. "Good morn. Are you ready to get this started?"

In unison, we answered, "Yes!"

"Good." He puffed on his cigar, then took a swig from his glass, which in an instant disappeared altogether. He clapped his hands. "Let's get started with the master of domain challenge."

He led us to the door we had entered, but this time when we stepped outside, things looked different. In front of us were seven glass coffins standing straight upwards. He waved his hand. "Each one of you will go inside one and stand there. Once inside you will have to endure that which you hate the most."

"How will you know what we dislike?" Griff asked.

"The dead know all," he replied eerily.

Saul leaned into my leg, and I looked at him. He gave me a one finger wave to kneel, then whispered in my ear. "You must win this challenge, or I fear Griff may put you on the block for expulsion."

I nodded. "Yeah, yeah," I retorted, taking a chance to look over at the dragon. He stretched out his wings and stuck his chest out. He cocked an eyebrow at me and grinned.

Baron Samedi broke through our Mexican standoff. "First things first, we must set some rules. Under no circumstances are you allowed to use any powers. We want to see if you are willing to live without them if you are lucky enough to win." His laugh chilled me to the bone. "When you've had enough you break the glass to get out." He grinned. Now if you do, you've lost the opportunity for power of the house."

I didn't know it then, but this skeletal man would continue to speak in riddles. As we all walked toward our glass tombs, the doors slid open. I turned and faced Baron Samedi and walked backward into my coffin. I sucked in a deep breath as the door closed with a click.

Before I could react, a small hole slid open in the side of my prison. I reached in and the cold silver burned my skin. Quickly I clenched it in my fist and held it. My attention focused on Mariwen to the left of me. She flapped her wings, holding her item. She didn't seem to be struggling too much. The others were...well, all except for Saul. He leaned back toward the back of his coffin. With one hand holding a small plant, the fingers of his other hand twirled his mustache. He glanced over at me and grinned wide.

I leaned back and took a deep breath. The silver burned my hand, searing into my skin. Looking over at Saul, I had to laugh when he tossed the plant from hand to hand and gave me the thumbs up sign. His assurance told me I could do this.

I closed my eyes, trying to erase the pain. Past thoughts plagued me....

"Look, son, you need to take responsibility. You're next to be alpha." My father spoke, never raising his voice.

I scoffed. "A responsibility I never wanted."

"Maxim, why do you speak like that?"

"Because I never wanted this." I waved my hands around.

"But you have no control over that. You were born into it; it's your birthright," he spoke irritably.

I shook my head. "Can't you get someone else? I know plenty who would gladly take my place."

He stood, growing angry at my defiance. "There will be no more talk of this nonsense. You will become alpha, and that is it."

I gripped the paper I held in my hand. As soon as my father left I smoothed out the paper and read.

Do you wish to be human?

If so, then we want you for an epic televised show. Where: The Zombie Lounge, New Orleans, LA When: Sunday, Oct 1, 2017, at midnight If you are chosen you will meet back at the Lafayette cemetery on All Hallows Eve!

I folded the flyer and shoved it back into my pocket. This was something I wanted to do...no, had to do.

The silver burned my hand and my eyes popped open. I looked around and saw three of the coffins empty, the glass shattered on the ground. Only four of us remained. Saul gave me the thumbs up and kicked at the glass entombing him. He dropped the plant and it sizzled into the dirt, disappearing. He walked over and sat with the others. Mariwen, Griff, and I remained.

I leaned back, letting the pain infuse my body. I popped an eye open and saw Mariwen struggling, but when I looked over at Saul he shook his head. Before I could make a move she pushed against her glass and it shattered. She flew out and dropped a small piece of iron. I just had to wait Griff out.

The silver now stung my skin, and I could smell my flesh burning. Just when I thought about giving up, Griff crashed out of his tomb and dropped a mirror onto the ground. The glass door to my coffin slid open and I dropped the silver. The ground swallowed it as Baron Samedi came over to me. Griff watched me, his anger evident on his face as he glowered at me.

"Congratulations, Maxim, you've won the honor of becoming master of domain. With it comes plenty of perks, but also responsibilities. Come inside." He smiled, revealing an almost chilling expression.

I glanced at Saul, who gave me a thumbs up. He ran forward and jumped on my shoulder. "Man, dude, I thought that big damn reptile would never concede."

I chuckled at his comment. "Me too."

Three

As we entered the house, Mariwen placed her hand on my shoulder, causing chills to engulf me. "Good job, Max." Her voice made me smile.

"Thank you, Mari." I figured if she could be ballsy enough to shorten my name, so could I. She sashayed into the house. Saul snickered at me, jumped from my shoulder, and ran into the house. Once we entered, in the middle of the room sat a huge fur carved throne, with marble steps leading up to it.

Saul tugged on my pants leg and whispered, "Oh shit, you may just have put a target on your back."

"Thanks for the tip off," I replied sarcastically. This was no surprise to me, though in all reality, the bulls-eye had probably been there since I stepped inside the house.

He shrugged, then chuckled. "You are welcome, my friend."

I shook my head at what I had gotten myself into. First, a desire to be human, and second, the desire for the fairy.

"Come, Maxim." Baron Samedi ushered me to the throne. I followed and sat. "Now, as part of your week-long reign, the others are here to serve you as you wish. You may choose one fellow creature to speak on your behalf. At the halfway mark you will choose two to be expelled from the house." He tipped his hat and smiled to the others. "But y'all have a chance to win your freedom. At the end of your week, there will be a vote, and one will be sent to the unknown. You will find your room has been updated to a suite."

I shook my head...must be the magic of this house. As soon as he finished he disappeared in a puff of smoke.

I glanced around at all the faces staring at me. I opened my mouth to speak, but Saul stopped me. "Could you please fix Maxim dinner while we talk?"

"I won't do a damn thing for the wolf," Griff bellowed.

Saul's eyes turned black and he stalked toward the dragon. "You'll do exactly what is requested of you per the loa of death's orders."

Mari walked forward. "Come on, Griff, you can watch while I cook." She glanced in my direction but quickly averted her eyes when Griff glared at her.

"Fine!" he grumbled and followed the others.

"I guess you're my second in command," I chuckled.

"Look, I had to jump in before you said something stupid," he joked.

"Why would you say that?" I narrowed my eyes.

He cocked a brow at me. "You were going to say something stupid, weren't you? Like, 'oh no, you don't have to serve me,'" he taunted me in a whiney voice.

I tilted my head and shrugged. "Maybe." I'd always hated the servitude that my werewolf pack had among its royalty.

Saul nudged me. "What is your plan, now that you are master of domain?"

I leaned further into the soft, fur covered throne, with my elbow on the armrest. "No idea."

He jumped up onto the back of the throne. His feet barely reached me at his height above me. His striped knee socks and black biker boots swung into my vision. "I think you must put Griff up on the chopping block, so to speak."

"I agree, but what if he wins the immunity challenge?"

"Then we must do everything in our power to not let that happen."

The others came toward me with trays full of food. Mariwen flew up the steps, never touching them with her dainty feet, and placed a tray beside me, then flittered off. She turned and looked over her shoulder at me and smiled. Part of me wondered if this was just a way of staying in my good graces. That little fairy had nothing to worry about. For a fleeting second, I thought about giving it all up for her.

Saul jumped down, landing one boot in my groin. I screamed in pain. "Fuck, Saul." I rubbed at the sore area.

He turned around, still standing on my lap. "You, my friend, will be a sitting duck if you keep your thoughts on that fairy. Now, let's eat this delicious dinner your subjects made for us," he chuckled.

"You go ahead."

He dug into the dinner, eating only the plants that I assumed Mari had put on the tray for him. My stomach growled, so I reached and grabbed a chicken leg. I sucked the meat off the bone effortlessly. The meat didn't sit well with me, making my stomach groan in protest. Once Saul was done, he looked up at me.

I snapped my fingers and Griff appeared. I turned to Saul and grinned. "Damn, I think I can get used to this," I taunted the dragon.

"What the hell do you—?"

"Griff, don't talk to your master of domain like that." Saul leaned back and chewed on his plant. Griff glared back at us and said nothing.

Saul stood up and stared at him. "What are you waiting for? Take this tray away."

Griff leaned in close to me. "Your little gnome friend can't keep you safe forever."

I stood, suddenly feeling an urge to rip his throat out. "I'd watch how you talk to me if I were you."

He matched my glare with the same anger. "I will not be at your beck and call for very long, wolf."

Saul stepped forward and pushed him back from me. I witnessed a red glow coming from his eyes. "You will do as you're instructed in the house or else."

Griff grabbed the tray and stalked off.

"Thanks, Saul."

"No, thank you," he replied and grinned.

My head began to pound causing me a sudden urge to vomit. I stood again but wavered a little, grabbing on to the armrest before I toppled down the marble stairs.

Saul looked pained at my apparent sickness. "How long did you hold the silver?"

"I don't know," I muttered incoherently.

"Why don't you get some sleep? I'll keep an eye out for any danger."

I stalked upstairs to my room. The pain in my hand alerted every nerve in my body. I leaned against the wall and sucked in a deep breath, willing my body to not explode from the pain... Saul kept close beside me.

30

When I stood in front of the door, it swung open to reveal Eloise jumping on the bed, her blonde pigtails flying in sync with her movements.

"What are you doing here, ghost?" Saul exclaimed.

She quit jumping and placed her hands on her hips. "I'm here to congratulate my new friend."

"Fine, but don't bother him too long, he needs his rest." Before he closed the door behind me, he said, "Don't let her outstay her welcome. Damn ghosts." Before the door shut, Eloise stuck her tongue out at Saul, who returned the gesture.

I cocked an eyebrow at him. "Very childish, Saul."

"She started it," he replied, shutting the door.

Eloise continued bouncing on the bed. "Hey, Maxi, you won," she squealed out in delight.

"I did." I mustered up a weak smile.

She stopped jumping as I sat on the bed. She glanced at my hand. "Maxi, does that hurt?" Her childlike squeal pierced my ears.

"Shhh, Eloise. Saul will hear you."

"Good, I hope he does. He's such a meany head."

I cocked an eyebrow at her. "He's not all that bad."

She gasped. "Uh, duh, yes he is...he's a gnome. They are mean little green boogers." She laughed at her joke.

I shook my head and leaned back on the pillow, cradling my hand. She plopped down beside me and whispered, "Does it hurt?"

I nodded. "It does."

Outside the door, a ruckus ensued. "No, you may not enter," Saul spoke with authority.

I didn't hear the reply...it was too low. So I adjusted my senses and concentrated.

"What is it, Maxi?" Eloise asked.

"Shh."

I concentrated more, finally hearing the sweet sound of Mariwen's voice. The door opened and there she stood a basket in her hand. "I can attend to his wounds."

Saul rolled his eyes. "Fine, but don't be putting any bullshit in his head. Fix his wounds, then leave."

I wondered what Saul's motives were as Mari entered. The scent of spring flowers wrapped around the room and she flew toward me. "Maxim, I can heal your wounds."

"Does Griff know you're here?"

She shook her head.

My chest tightened as she came closer. In my ear, I heard Eloise singing *Mari and Maxi sitting in a tree k i s s i n g....* I tuned her out and focused on the fairy, who sat on the edge of the bed.

"Let me see your hand."

I did as she asked, holding out my hand. She gasped loudly.

"Why are you helping me?" I asked.

She reached into her basket, then sighed. "It's what I have been trained for all my life. All fairies have a gift...mine is healing." She gripped my hand in hers. Her soft touch sent an electrical pulse throughout my body. I sucked in a breath, then slowly let it out. Her hair was tied up in a nice neat bun on top, but a few stray strands fell in her face, and she peeked at me through them. I reached my hand out to brush a stray blonde strand from her face, but before I could she blew at it and tucked it behind her ear. Quickly, I dropped my hand. Every touch sent my nerves into hyperdrive. What the hell was happening to me?

Eloise whispered in my ear. "That's easy, silly, you like her. She's pretty. You should take her on a date like my dad used to with my mom." She giggled in my ear.

I laughed and Mari looked up at me. "What's so funny?" she asked.

"Nothing."

She eyed me. "Sure. Now be still, this is going to hurt. The silver poison has shifted its way into your bloodstream." She stood from the bed and went to the bathroom with her little basket. "I'll be right back. I need to make a poultice to place on the wound."

I drifted off to sleep waiting for Mari to return. In my ear, Eloise read a children's book to me. I woke to a coldness being placed in the palm of my hand. The paste-like substance caked into my skin.

"It will only take a few minutes for the paste to pull the poison out," she comforted me. Then the pain of it being sucked out of me brought tears to my eyes, and sweat beaded on my forehead. Eloise dropped her book. She returned with a cold compress, draping it across my head. Her tiny hands were careful not to get water in my eyes. "Maxi, please don't die," she cried softly.

"I won't," I promised her. Soon I closed my eyes once again, keeping my ears alert.

Mari's hands shook while she wrapped a material around my hand. The wet paste pressed into my skin and cooled the burning on my palm.

"This will help get any residual poison out. Max, I'm also making you some tea. Please drink it, it will stop the fever from staying. I'll leave some extra with Saul."

I leaned back and grabbed her hand in mine. "Thank you for helping me, Mari."

"You are welcome." She patted my leg.

As I slipped in and out of consciousness, voices whispered in my ear. "Will he be okay?" Saul asked.

"Yes."

"Good," he replied.

One other thing...he will have a lasting scar where my concoction drew out the poison. My magic will get rid of this poison, but make sure he gets plenty of rest and liquid to push out any residual silver still in his body. I'm leaving some tea...make sure he drinks it. It'll help."

I drifted into a deep sleep as the door closed. Throughout the night, as the toxins were pulled from my body, the pain intensified. At one point, I woke screaming. Eloise lay nestled beside me, her little ghostly hands clutching at the book on her chest. I didn't think ghosts slept, but maybe it was her way of coping. Sweat beaded on my forehead, sending chills all over me. I sat and looked around.

In the corner in a leather chair Mari was curled up, her long hair covering her face, her wings folded around her petite body. As I gazed at the fairy, the pain subsided. I looked for Saul, who I found leaning against Mari's chair, his red hat covering a portion of his face. I smiled, knowing the gnome was looking out for all of us, so I drifted back to sleep.

Four

I woke to the sound of voices speaking in hushed tones, so I stirred a little and they stopped. I no longer sensed Mari in the room. I held my breath and they continued. "Saul, I asked for one thing from you. One thing."

"Zora, what was I supposed to do, let him lose?"

I stilled as Saul and the cat talked about me. "He could have died."

"But he didn't. Damn that dragon, I didn't think he could hold out as long. I mean, for a dragon to look at himself in a mirror and see his vulnerability for that long is mind-blowing."

"Well, do better," she purred. The bed dipped slightly as the cat jumped on. "Go get some rest. I'll keep an eye on him. Better yet, go listen to the others and see what they are doing."

He didn't speak as he left. When the door closed, I popped an eye open. Zora lay curled at the foot of the bed.

"Maxim, ask your questions."

A dozen or so questions popped into my head, but only one popped out. "Why are you really here?"

She uncurled her body, stretched, and sat, licking her paw in a normal cat-like reaction. "Your father reached out to my family for help."

I sat quickly. "What do you mean?" I asked, full of curiosity.

"I come from a long line of familiars. We are known to specifically protect good paranormal creatures, so he went to the two covens here in New Orleans and asked for help."

My brain couldn't concentrate on this news. "Wait..." I couldn't believe what I was hearing, "he didn't want me...."

She padded over to me and sat beside me, her tail swishing on the bed. "He's still your father. He loves you. A good father only wants his son to be happy. Besides, he didn't want anything bad to happen to you."

Someone interrupted us, knocking on the door. "May I come in?"

"Yes," I said.

The door opened and Vanity entered, carrying a tray laden with tons of food. "We thought you'd be hungry after your ordeal." She glided over to me, placing the tray on the bed.

Zora hissed at her, but all she did was wave the cat off. Zora reciprocated by swatting at her with claws extended.

"Shit," Vanity yelled in pain.

I shook my head at Zora. "No."

"Well she asked for it."

The elf glared at the feline. "Where did it come from?"

She stood and stalked the elf. "I'm not an 'it.'"

"Oh great, the 'it' talks," she said sarcastically, but turned her attention back to me. I smiled thinking Zora would retaliate, like any other cat would, by shredding something of Vanity's.

"I'll be back if you need me," Zora said as she leapt off the bed and stalked outside. "Be careful of the pointy-eared one."

Vanity turned back to me as soon as the cat left. "Why does she not like you?" I asked Vanity.

She shrugged. "Elves and familiars haven't gotten along in years. I don't really remember why, but I think it's a feud that has existed for centuries."

"Hmm." I didn't press the matter, thinking maybe I'd find out eventually.

"So, how are you feeling, Maxim? Much better, I hope?"

The door opened and Saul walked in and jumped onto the bed. "Hello, Vanity, how's it going? Have you brought our master his breakfast, or are you trying to talk game with him?" he sneered.

"Well, if everyone would leave us alone I *could* talk game."

"Not without me." He plopped on the bed, revealing red striped socks on his feet. "Are you proposing an alliance with my man here?" He sat on the bed, his arms crossed over his chest. Silver skull rings adorned his fingers. I'd never seen them on him before.

She tossed her ebony hair over her shoulder and smiled at him. "Well you know, an alliance can take us only so far."

"Yes, I know," he said. "First things first. Vanity, can I ask you what the item was you held in your hand for the comp?"

She brushed a hand over her hair and contemplated her reply. "Why?"

He stood and walked across the bed to her. "Because I want to know what is your kryptonite, so to speak."

She sighed. "A dragon's tooth. It's poisonous to elves."

He nodded and sat. She eyed him and cocked her head at him. "Don't think you can use that against me at a later date little weed."

He feigned a look of shock. "I have no idea what you mean."

I pushed myself off the bed and wobbled back and forth. "I'll agree to an alliance on one condition; we add Mari to this little group."

Vanity laughed. "I doubt that will happen...she's already aligned with Griff."

"Only because he has something on her," Eloise spoke up and floated over to us.

"How do you know?" I asked her.

She widened her eyes in shock, then laughed. "Because silly, I've been snooping in the house."

"Wait, they could catch you." A sudden concern for her sucker punched me.

"Nuh uh." She shook her head vigorously. "They can't see me unless I want them to," she snickered.

"Shit...."

"Oh no, Maxi, you said a naughty word." She pointed her finger at me disapprovingly.

Saul grinned and looked apologetic for me.

I laughed. "I'm sorry, Ely."

"Oooh, you gave me a nickname." She squealed with delight and clapped her hands.

Saul waved his hands. "Come on, we have a game to play here. Let's get our heads into it."

I eyed him. "We have to protect Mari from Griff."

"Spoken like a true alpha," Saul retorted.

"Yeah, yeah." I ignored his comment. "We don't want Griff to know of our plan to bring Mari to our alliance."

"How do you plan on getting her to agree?"

I laughed out loud. "I'll appeal to her good nature. Ely, would you like to help me?"

She nodded. "How?"

"Will you agree to show yourself to Mari so we can talk to her?"

She rocked back and forth, digging the toe of her bare foot into the carpet. "Uh, I don't know, Maxi."

"Come on, you showed yourself to Vanity." I smiled, prodding her to help us.

She gazed at the elf and smiled. "Because she's pretty, and not aligned with that ugly ole dragon." Vanity smiled back at the ghost. Ely leaned in close to me. "His breath smells, too." She covered her mouth and giggled.

"Don't you think Mari is pretty too?"

She thought for a second. "Yes." She blushed. "But she's with that ugly old scaly mean dragon."

"We know that's not her fault." I cocked my head at her.

She pondered this for a second. "Okay, I'll help you."

"Do you really think this is a good idea?" Saul asked.

I cocked a brow at him. "Come on, Saul, I saw you keeping an eye on her last night. I swear I won't tell anyone you aren't a total hard ass."

"Good." He looked at Vanity. "Elf, you keep your mouth shut, or—"

"Or what, little garden weed?" she laughed.

I interrupted them. "Good, then it's settled. Vanity, can you go see if Mari will come join us here?"

"How do I get her away from Griff?"

"Tell her that not all the poison is out and I need her. Saul will guard the door if he tries anything."

She nodded and glided out of the room. As soon as she did Ely and Saul looked at me. "Do you trust the elf?" they both asked in unison.

"No, not really. Though we do need numbers." I shrugged.

"Now that's more like it, thinking game." He grinned wide.

I kept my thoughts to myself. It was all about protecting Mari.

"Before they come back let's talk about who we want to nominate," Saul asked.

"One second." I walked over to the bathroom, leaving the door open. I turned on the faucet and splashed cold water on my face. When I glanced back at them, they were looking at me, waiting for an answer. "First, let's put up Griff and the goblin."

"And hope Griff doesn't win the immunity challenge," Saul said.

Just then Mari and Vanity walked inside. Mari held the little basket over her arm. "Hey, can y'all leave us for a bit?"

Saul nodded his head. "Come on, Vanity." They both exited the room.

"Vanity said the poison is still in your body."

"Here, sit." I patted the bed.

The fairy sat on the bed and held her basket in her lap. "I was sure that all the poison would've been removed." She grabbed my hand and unwrapped the bandage. Her soft touch on my palm sent jolts through me. "I don't get it. It looks okay."

I grabbed her hand in mine. "Mari, tell me what Griff has on you."

She pulled from my grasp. "What do you mean?"

Eloise appeared and Mari gasped. "Don't be afraid, Miss Mari," Eloise said. "Please tell Maxi here what the dragon has on you."

Her eyes began to well with silvery glistening tears sliding down her cheeks. "I can't."

I touched her face as she dropped her head. "Yes, you can. You're safe with us."

Eloise sat beside her. "This is my father's house. As long as you're here, Griff can't hurt you."

Mari sniffed back some tears. "My brother got into trouble a while back. Even King Roi doesn't know what we did." She wiped the tears away and hiccupped. "Princess Alicia wasn't the only one to escape to the human world. After she crossed over the veil, he went as a sentry in search of her. It was something they were forbidden to do—"

"Why?" I interrupted her.

She laughed, but quickly covered her mouth. "Because we are protected by our magic. If we leave the safety of our realm we forget who we are."

I glanced at her. "But you've left the realm...how do you still have your memories?"

She pulled a chain out from under her clothes. A beautiful stone dangled from it, sparkling a bright blue-green. "I got this from a voodoo priestess in the bayou. Same reason I've kept my wings."

Eloise gasped. "I've heard of her. Her name is Cassandra. Even Marie Laveau herself vouches for her powers."

Mari smiled. "Yes. She is kind to all paranormal creatures. Anyway, we informed her of the deal my parents made with Griff to protect my brother. At first, she wanted us to tell King Roi, but my brother would have been banished from our realm for disobeying an order." She started to cry again.

"Don't cry, Mari. We'll help you," I tried to comfort her.

She wiped at her eyes. "You can't. Our payment for helping my brother is that I must marry Griff. Though I'm not totally sure what his ulterior motive could be. I just know I don't want to win the thought of losing who I am is devastating." She fiddled with the amulet. "Cassandra gave me this to keep the illusion while I'm in the house. We don't want Griff to know all of our secrets." She started to sob uncontrollably. "I don't want to be human; I want to remain a fairy."

Suddenly my heart broke for her but vowed to help her escape from Griff. "Don't worry, we have a plan to get him out of the house."

She glanced at me, her face all red and blotchy from crying. "Really?"

"Yes." I nodded and wiped a lone tear that trickled down her face. Her soft skin ignited my own. "I'll put him up for expulsion."

"What if he wins immunity?" she questioned me.

"We have to make sure that doesn't happen," I reassured her.

She hugged me, and as her head pressed against my chest the scent of magnolias and warm summer sun invaded my nostrils.

"I'll do whatever I can to protect you." I paused and held her at arm's length. "You must promise me something."

She nodded. "Anything."

"You have to act like you know nothing of our plan. Dragons have an uncanny sense of sniffing out betrayal. I would rather that fall on me."

She shook her head. "I don't know if I can."

After I'd pulled her back towards me, I tipped her chin up as she dropped her head. "You can. I'm afraid if he finds out, you won't be safe."

"Mari, you can do it...I'll be by your side. Griff will never see me," Eloise spoke, holding a doll. "Even Suzie will help." She shoved the doll in her face. Mari laughed slightly and stood.

"If y'all have faith in me, I can too."

Eloise clapped her hands. "Yay, Mari." She dropped her doll, grabbed the fairy's hand, and danced around her, and Mari giggled. The sound pierced my heart and a wave of happiness I'd never experienced coursed through me. I stood and glanced at Eloise. "May I cut in?"

She giggled. "Sure."

She handed me Mari's hand that she held, and I took her in my arms. Music magically played from somewhere in the distance. I pulled her closer to me and rocked my hips. She rested her head on my chest.

Before the song ended, I dipped her low placing a soft kiss on her nose. She blushed a deep red. I pulled her back up and kept my arms around her.

The door swung open and Griff stormed in. "What the hell is going on here?"

Mari pulled away from me as Saul ran in behind the dragon. "Nothing...," Mari stuttered.

Mari hurried out, followed closely by Griff.

Saul stalked toward me. "Damn. I tried to stop him, but he threatened to burn down the house."

"It's okay. We just have to keep an eye on Mari with him." I proceeded to fill him on the predicament.

Five

After a day or so of recuperation from my poison, I woke to a renewed focus on the game. It was to protect Mari at all costs. With my head in my hands, I thought about the big decision I had to make.

A crack resounded in my room, and there stood Baron Samedi. "Good morning, Maxim. How are you feeling?" He stood back, eyeing me as if wondering if I was going to make it.

I glanced at him and smiled weakly. "You didn't tell us we would almost die in that competition."

He glared, his eyes turning a bright crimson but then changing back to black. "Do not question the game. You signed up for this, did you not?" he snarled.

"Yes, I did."

He took out a cigar from his tuxedo pocket and magically it lit. He puffed on it, then left it dangling from his mouth. "One will sacrifice everything for something they want badly enough, don't you agree?"

I nodded in agreement. Now I feared I would be sacrificing my need of wanting to be human to keep Mari safe.

"Well, Maxim, have you decided who you will be nominating to be expelled from the house?"

"I have." Confidence was rolling off me in waves.

"Very well." He handed me a small black marble coffin. "There are voodoo dolls representing all of y'all. Please place the ones that you want to be nominated for expulsion in the coffin."

"Where will I find the dolls?"

"Here." A huge armoire that had previously not been there opened, revealing seven dolls that represented the seven of us. "Be careful in the decision you make. When you are ready, join us in the great hall." He tipped his hat and grinned.

He left in a haze of smoke, and I went over to the dolls. Each one represented each one of us, even me. I gently touched the one resembling Mari with one finger. Quickly I grabbed the two dolls I wanted for the ceremony and shut them into the marble coffin. "That should do it," I muttered under my breath.

The lights in the room dimmed. A crackling sound emanated around me.

I took a deep breath and walked out of my room, descended the steps, and entered the great hall, where everyone else sat on a marble bench against the wall, waiting for my announcement. Baron stood off to the side, leaning against one of the pillars at the back of the room. In the middle of the black wall hung a macabre marble gothic architecture. On each side sat a skull, and in the middle a glass case with a deep red material covering the back. Tiny spikes lined the bottom of the piece. Flanking this piece on each side was a sconce, each holding a different size candle. Tiny flames flickered on each candle, illuminating the small room. They also gave an eerie shadow over the skeletal face of our host.

To my left, a wooden table sat parallel to the bench. Baron Samedi strode over to me as I entered holding the coffin. For the first time, I heard the cameras in the room clicking and moving around, no doubt to catch a glimpse of who I was nominating.

"Ladies and gentlemen, this is our first selection ceremony. Maxim, please place the coffin on the table behind you, and tell us who you've chosen and why."

I sucked in a breath and let it out slowly. As I placed the coffin on the table, I turned to face the others. I opened it and picked my first doll. "First I've chosen Corbin." The doll slid from my hand and balanced in the air. Then what I said next sealed my fate in the house. "You are not my target." I scooped up the other doll and held it out. "Second, I choose Griff." The doll floated into the air beside Corbin's.

Before I could say why the dragon lunged at me. "You asshole."

I growled at him, trying to shift so it could be somewhat of a fair fight. The hair started to grow along my arm, and my canines began to extend. "Get off me." I pushed him back and watched as he erupted into scales. Saul ran over to him, latching onto his leg with his teeth. Griff glanced down and shook him off. Saul skidded across the floor, bumping into the wall. Mari ran over to him to check on him. He let her check him over, but he scowled the entire time.

My anger surfaced and I growled. Above us, the glass pendeloques on the black gothic chandelier clanked together. A few of the tiny candles tipped over and dropped wax on the floor, then the candles fell to the floor.

"Leave my friends out of this."

A loud thumping echoed off the walls. Baron stood there, his staff banging on the hardwood floors. "Enough! Maxim's decision has been made." He turned to Griff. "You'll have a chance to win your freedom in two days. In the meantime, accept your fate or else."

Griff shifted back to human and stalked toward me. Inches from my face, he snarled, "I will win that immunity, and you, wolf, are my next target."

I walked over to Saul and helped him up. Facing Griff, I retorted, "Challenge accepted," growling loudly.

"Come with me!" He grabbed Mari and dragged her off. Her soft sobs followed her as she left us.

"I'm worried about her."

Saul dusted himself off. "Don't worry, we just need to make sure he doesn't win that damned immunity." The others retreated and left the room.

Corbin walked over to us and offered me his hand. "Look, no ill will toward you for the nom, dude. I know it's just a game. But," he leaned in closer, "Griff is not going to be easy to get out. The rumors are he is some sort of big bad guy."

"We've heard, but it just means we need to fight to get him out."

He nodded as he stalked off.

"Holy shit," Saul exclaimed, not even trying to hide his snicker. I turned around and watched as Zora strolled in with a baby bonnet on her head, her expression laced with dissatisfaction.

"Please stop this child. I'm a cat, not a baby." She sat, trying to remove the hat with her paw but with no luck.

"Maxi, don't you like Zora's new hat?"

I stifled a laugh and knelt. "The question is, does Zora like her new hat?" I cocked my head at her. "I don't think she does."

The cat sat there stewing over having the ghost child dress her as a baby. Eloise glanced back to the cat and started to cry. "Oh no, Zora doesn't like it."

I glanced over at the cat, who glared at me. "Come on, Zora, tell her you like it." I winked at her.

The cat huffed. "Oh, all right. I like the hat, Eloise," she stuttered out.

The little ghost clapped her hands in joy, scooped up the cat in her arms, and squealed with delight. She squeezed Zora so hard the cat had to do her best not to claw the child's eyes out, which would have been quite difficult with Eloise being a ghost and all.

Six

I shuffled out into the kitchen, and what I saw gave me an idea. Mari stood at the sink humming and dancing to the music floating through the house. Her hips swayed and her wings fluttered, causing her to rise from the floor. Knowing the house had a magical allure to it, I hoped it would help me out. I thought long and hard about what music I'd like the house to play. My Spanish heritage had taught me to dance quite well. So, when the house obliged me by playing the perfect song, I let the music fuel my soul and body.

Mari turned and her lips pulled at the corner of her mouth. "What are you doing, Max?"

"Come dance with me." I enticed her toward me. "Let my magical hips take you to a faraway land," I laughed.

She shook her head. "I can't. Griff may walk in any moment."

"Well then, let's make the most of our time dancing." Inching closer, I took her hand and twirled her around, then moved my hips in sync to the tunes. I grinned as she let go of her inhibitions and moved with me, letting me lead her on the floor. The song moved me, and the closer I held her a feeling I couldn't explain wrapped around me.

"Hey, you two had better stop." Vanity walked in, interrupting our closeness. "Griff is awake."

Mari pulled from my embrace and dropped her head. "Thanks for the dance."

Placing a finger under her chin I caused her to stare into my eyes. "You are welcome, fair lady."

As I turned around Griff entered and glared at me. Baron Samedi entered in a puff of smoke. "Good morning. Are you ready for the immunity challenge?"

Griff stepped forward, nudging me hard with his shoulder. "Let's do this. I'm ready to win my freedom."

Saul rolled his eyes. As Griff walked forward the gnome stuck out his boot, and the dragon tripped and stumbled forward. He jumped forward and turned on us. "Who the hell did that?"

Saul shook his head. "No idea, dude. Maybe your shoes are too big and you tripped over them. You should watch where you walk."

He roared loudly. "You, little punk ass, better watch yourself."

"Or what?" Saul replied, and lunged forward. I held him back. "Not now."

Baron Samedi glanced in my direction and smiled. "Let's all head outside."

We followed him. The cool air hit us the moment we stepped out of the house. I glanced around and tried to adjust my eyes to the pitch darkness. Off in the distance, I could see the tops of cement tombs. I tried to focus my eyes, but Baron Samedi walked up and placed a hand on my shoulder.

He shook his head. "No using powers or your senses." This would not be an easy task.

"Okay. At the other end of this cemetery is a glowing orb, one that emits a dark crimson color. But there are others that are deceiving. If you bring back the wrong one you must start over. If you receive the one with a skull within then you immediately lose. The first one to complete this task in the least amount of time wins immunity. Now on the way, you will encounter things that wish you not to reach your ultimate goal. Now, everyone go back inside and return to your own rooms. I'll call you one by one. When you're done please return to the great hall."

We filed back inside the house and waited to be called. I slowly ascended the steps to my room. Once inside I was greeted by Zora and Eloise, both curled up on my bed. Ely petted Zora and the cat's eyes were shut tight.

I sat on the bed and waited for my turn. The tension in the room matched what was happening inside me. I glanced at the gothic clock on the wall, which read five o'clock. "Damn, it's been two hours."

Finally, a raspy voice echoed through the room. "Maxim, please exit the house, it's your turn to compete," Baron requested.

I stood and shoved my hands into my pockets.

Eloise jumped up, knocking Zora to the floor. The cat meowed and hissed as she clutched at the bed. Her claws tore into the fabric as she tried to regain her composure. "Sorry, Zora." Ely helped her back on the bed. Then she faced me and hugged me. "Good luck, Maxi."

"Thank you, Ely."

I left and headed down the hallway. Before I got to the stairs, Mari popped into view. She grabbed my hand and pulled me from the view of the cameras.

"What are you doing?"

She pushed her glasses further onto her nose. "I wanted to wish you good luck and give you this." She stood on her tiptoes and kissed me on the cheek, then shoved a small knife into my hand. I didn't see how such a tiny thing would help, but I shoved it in my pocket, then disappeared in a flash down the steps. My fingers traced over the spot where her lips had made contact with my skin. I grinned and headed outside for my turn.

Baron Samedi met me outside. "Are you ready, Maxim?"

I nodded. "Yes, sir."

"Good. Your time starts now."

I ran off in the direction I hoped the orb was located. The ground grew wet and muddy as I made my way through, and I fell in the muck. My hands gripped the ground but found only thick mud. With every movement, I became more imprisoned. My fingers grasped at the ground again, and with some luck, I pulled myself free.

As I pushed up from the dirt, I steadied, trying not to fall again. I waited for my legs to not give out. Once I regained my strength I ran toward my goal, but an invisible force came at me. The scent of fresh decay infused with all the other smells. I looked around, searching for the cause, even though my surroundings were death.

Then I saw it...a zombie. It growled and chomped at me, trying to stop me from my mission. I tussled with it, and it tried its best to eat me. After a few minutes, I reached around and grabbed the back of its head, and pulled and pulled until the tendons ripped from his neck. I threw it to the ground and it rolled away from me. I wiped my hands on my jeans, wiping the blood and guts off.

I searched the area for anything else trying to stop me. Then out of nowhere, a huge oak tree branch knocked me to the ground. I couldn't breathe, and when the air came back into my lungs I kept low and crawled across the soft dirt. From my position, I saw a dozen or so orbs up ahead, all in a knee-high pile. I ran faster but was thrown back by an invisible force. I blinked, trying to focus on things, but still didn't see what had knocked me on the ground.

The skies opened and the rain pelted all around n me. My long hair became drenched and stuck to me. I tried to brush it back, but couldn't. My vision blurred and I wiped at my eyes with mud covered hands. "Shit!" I screamed in frustration. One more time I tried to stand up, then took a deep breath and focused. As I saw a blur of an object fly at me, I dodged out of the way and ran to the orbs. Hastily I began digging around for the right one. Carefully I took my time, making sure I did not receive the one with the skull inside. But they all looked the same. How in the hell would I find the right one? I shook my head, sighed, and tried again to pull my hair into a bun.

Once my hair was out of my face I continued the search. I carefully searched each one for a hint of what I needed. I picked up one and could see a tiny skull deep inside. I tossed it aside and kept looking. Finally, I found one with a deep crimson color in the middle. With a strong confidence I'd chosen the correct one, I stood. Sucking in a deep breath I ran, but the invisible thing that had attacked me before knocked me back to the ground again, but this time it kept me prisoner. I struggled against its hold.

"How in the hell do I fight something like this?" I screamed out loud. Then I remembered the item Mari had given me. I shifted my body slightly and dug into my pocket. Pulling out the small knife, my reflection shimmered in the shiny iron. I sliced at the invisibility holding me down. When I made contact, it shrieked and let me go.

Before it had a chance to attack, again I ran straight for Baron Samedi. As I reached him, I bent over and breathed heavily. Sweat dripped down my face and I wiped it away.

"Did you find the right one?" He held out his hand and I placed the orb in it.

"I sure as hell hope so. I don't think I can deal with what's out there again."

The loa flipped the orb around and a deep crimson fog filled the entire thing. "Good job, Maxim. Now head back inside and wait for me to enter after the last contestant."

I did as he instructed and went to the great hall and waited with the others. About an hour later, Baron Samedi appeared.

"All right, let's find out who has won immunity."

Griff stood with arms crossed and a huge grin plastered on his face. Saul nudged me. "I don't like the look on his face."

From the corner of my eye, I could see his pompous demeanor. "I don't either."

Before us appeared a scoreboard. Our names were on it, and beside them were small black drapes. "All right. You had a time of...," with a wave of his hand the small drape fell away, "four minutes, Corbin, but you brought back the wrong orb. I'm sorry, you are eliminated." He puffed on his cigar. "Next, Sally, you have a time of five minutes, and you brought back the correct orb. You are in first place." She grinned wide and flipped her hair over her shoulder. "Saul, you have a time of two minutes and also have brought back the correct orb."

Griff's name was next and his smile grew. I nudged Saul. "There is no way he beat my score."

Griff glanced in our direction and smiled. Baron Samedi waved the little drape from his time and a hush fell over the rest of us.

"It can't be!" Mari exclaimed.

"With a time of one minute and fifteen seconds, Griff, you are in first place." The rest of the times were a blur as I realized there was no way I had beaten him. "Maxim, you have a total of one minute and twenty-five seconds." As the final scores were revealed my stomach became queasy at the realization he had won immunity.

"Congratulations, Griff, you've won immunity. Maxim, you now must nominate a replacement for expulsion."

What the hell was I going to do? An invisible force pulled me back to my room. When I opened the door Eloise ran over to me. "Maxi, did you win, huh, huh?"

Zora padded over to us. "Eloise, I don't think he did. Can you go read your book, please?"

"But...." She started to protest but Zora glared at her. She huffed and left.

With my target safe, I had to choose a new one. That wasn't the problem; the fact that Griff would not be going home bothered me. Saul stormed in, letting the door bounce off the wall and swing back shut.

"That asshole cheated. It's the only way he could have won." He sauntered over to the bed and slapped me on the back. "We'll get him next time."

Eloise floated into the room in a hurry. "I've got news."

Saul interrupted her. "So, I suggest nominating Sally as a replacement, and let the vote's fall where they do. Besides I don't like her."

Eloise tugged on Saul's hat. "I've got news," she bellowed out. He turned around.

"What is it?"

She stuck her tongue out at him and faced me. "Griff did cheat."

"I knew it," Saul said smugly, crossing his arms over his chest.

"How do you know?"

She grinned. "I eavesdropped on him talking to the goblin and the selkie."

"What did he say?" I asked.

"He said he cheated, duh."

I cocked my head at her. "How?"

"Ohhhh, that." She drawled out the words, then giggled. "He said he had something that could call the right orb to him from a distance. He didn't go that far into the cemetery. Instead, he stood off by a tree and called the orb to him."

"Damn it," Saul hollered.

"Hey, Mr. Saul said a bad word," Eloise tattled. This caused laughter from the gnome, the first I'd ever heard from him. Eloise looked at the both of us. "What's so funny?"

"Nothing." I knelt. "Eloise, please promise me you will be careful around Griff."

She nodded, but then looked doe-eyed at me. "I will, but he can't hurt me. I'm already dead, silly."

"Yeah, yeah. True." I smiled and patted her on the head.

Saul paced around in a circle. "The damn dragon, shit it was obvious he cheated, he didn't have an ounce of mud or dirt on him." Saul stood stone-faced, full of anger. Eloise floated over and tugged a leaf from Saul's hat.

I chuckled. "Okay Ely, can you go grab Vanity and ask her to come to my room?"

She nodded, dropped the leaf, and dashed through the door.

Minutes later, Vanity opened the door. She sat in a chair across from me, her long legs crossed at the ankle. "So, what's the plan now?"

I re-tied my hair up in a man bun and pushed my glasses back onto my nose. "Well, obviously I need to nominate someone else."

"I say put the selkie up. It's the obvious choice. We know they are working with Griff," Vanity hinted.

"I'm going to suggest we vote Corbin off. But we need to keep it from Mari so Griff doesn't suspect her of working with us," I told them.

Saul stood, his anger still apparent, "I'm going to get a bite to eat. Would you like something?" he asked me.

"Sure, some cookies and cream ice cream with peanut butter." I reached out to him. "Don't do anything stupid, please."

"Like what?" he asked.

I cocked my head. "Like mess with Griff."

He tipped his hat and I saw a hint of a Mohawk underneath. "I'm at your service, but I can't promise the latter." He chuckled out loud and left.

Seven

The next few hours consisted of waiting. I had a decision to make, and I just wanted Griff out of the house. But as the world had seen that was not going to happen now.

Saul walked in. "Are you ready to make your announcement?"

I nodded. "I guess so."

As soon as my choice of a replacement was announced, we would have the live expulsion ceremony. I somberly descended the steps to where everyone waited for me. Griff had his arm wrapped tightly around Mari's shoulders. Saul pulled me back as my body tensed, wanting to go to her. "Not now, my friend." My body constricted at wanting to tear the dragon limb from limb.

Over in the corner, I saw Baron Samedi. He smiled as soon as he saw me and glided over to me, staff in hand. "Have you made your decision, Maxim?"

"Yes, I have."

He grinned wide, showing all his white, pearly teeth. "Tell me."

I took in a deep breath and sighed. "Sally, I'm sorry, but I have to nominate you in Griff's spot." She glowered at me with an angry expression.

Baron Samedi clapped his hands. "It is done. Now I'll give you all a few minutes to decide who will be leaving here forever." He cackled and ushered me over to the huge throne, where I sat. Baron Samedi stood beside me, his staff in hand. "Okay, let's get this started."

Before us on a table sat a fine marble coffin. Baron blew smoke toward it, and a skeletal hand formed in the haze and reached for the box. It clicked it open and the lid flew open. Inside sat the two voodoo dolls I had chosen the other day. In a flash Griff's voodoo doll vanished and Sally's replaced it.

"Let the voting begin." Baron Samedi raised his hand and waved Vanity over to the box.

With her back to us, she picked up a doll and a pin. She faced us and stuck the pin in the doll. Mari was next. She faced us with a different doll and stuck the pin inside. She laid it gently back on the table and wiped a tear away. She didn't want any of this. I wanted to comfort her but held back from going to her. Baron Samedi nodded at Saul to go and place his vote. He chose the same doll as Vanity, sliding a pin into the material of the doll. Griff stalked over to the table, a huge grin planted on his face, and made his vote.

The loa of the dead hit his staff against the steps. "It looks as if we have a tie, which means you must be the deciding vote." He turned to me. I glared at Griff. He'd voted that way on purpose. Baron interrupted my thoughts. "So who will it be?"

I stood and descended the steps, picked up the doll, and voted with my alliance.

"It has been decided. I'm sorry, but Corbin has been expelled from the house. Get your bag and follow me outside." Corbin didn't look happy that he was being sent packing. Saul sat on the back of my chair. He slapped his hands together then raised one. "He's outta here."

As Corbin left the house with Baron Samedi, Griff eyed me and mouthed, "You're next."

Saul walked up to him. "Don't threaten him."

He leered at Saul. "Then you'd better make sure you or he wins."

"We will."

"Good luck."

Saul jumped onto the table beside Griff. "We know you cheated during the immunity comp."

Griff's expression grew angry but quickly shifted to faux shock. "What are you talking about? I won that fair and square."

Saul cocked a brow at him. "Yeah, sure you did." Sarcasm rolled off his tongue.

Griff crossed his arms over his chest. "Believe what you want, but your friend over there is next." He stalked off but turned to look over his shoulder. "And Maxim...." He enunciated each word. "Stay away from Mariwen. She belongs to me."

I lunged forward but Vanity stopped me. "No, Maxim, don't let him get into your head." She scowled at Griff.

He waved us off. "You all go have your fun. Though I promise you, I'll get each one of you out of this house." He continued on his way out of the room. He grabbed Mari by the shoulder and she pulled back slightly. He looked over at me then back to her. "He'd better not be putting ideas in your head. The entire fairy realm is in my hands."

She sobbed silently and followed him out of the room.

"Damn, I dislike that guy." I slammed my fist on the table, causing it to jump a few inches from the floor.

"Max." Saul looked at me. For the first time, his expression showed compassion. "Keep your head. You can't keep her safe if you aren't in the house."

I nodded. "You know that asshole will nominate me next if he wins."

He bowed his head. "I know, damn it. And he will likely cheat as well to do it."

"True." I shook my head.

He patted me on the back. "Let's go play a game of chess."

I followed him and Vanity but tried to think of ways to steal moments with Mari without Griff's knowledge.

We sat at the marble chess set. The pieces slid to their proper places. I eyed Saul as he removed his hat. In seconds, the hat turned into a ball cap. "What the hell?" he exclaimed.

I leaned back and laughed out loud. "The house is magical, remember?"

He scowled at me but replaced the hat backward on his head. He smoothed out his beard. "Let's play."

The next few hours proved futile. From our position as we played chess, we had a perfect view of the house. It angered me to watch the way Griff kept a close eye on Mari. Every time she got even a small distance away from him he'd tug her back closer to him. I returned my focus back to Saul and the game when I sensed him glaring at me.

"Just hurry and make a move so I can win the game," he snickered at me.

I contemplated my next move, but with my mind on other things, I couldn't concentrate on the game. So I made a move that would cost me to forfeit the game. Saul cocked a brow at me, then grinned. "Checkmate." He leaned back, took off his hat, and stared at it as it returned to its natural shape. He then placed it back on his head. "Why don't you go check on your girl?"

"Are you sure?"

He nodded. "Yep, I want to tour the house a little more."

Eight

I descended the steps, but Griff and Mari had disappeared. So I opened the freezer and pulled out a container of ice cream, scooped out some, and placed it in a bowl. Finding a spoon, I stuck it into the frozen concoction and swayed my hips from side to side as I danced to one of the barstools. I planted my ass down and sighed deeply, remembering the time I'd danced with Mari. As I sat eating cookies and cream ice cream I devised a plan.

Vanity strode into the kitchen, her long skirt trailing behind her.

"Vanity, can I speak to you for a moment, please?"

"Sure, sugar. Let me grab some water and we can chat." I finished the last of the ice cream and put the bowl into the sink. She smiled at me.

Saul met us on the steps. "Where ya going?"

"Talk. I want you to join us too."

His expression showed concern as he eyed me quizzically. "Sure."

Once in my room, I sat on the bed and the elf sat across from me. "What's on your mind?" Vanity asked as she crossed her long legs.

"I want you to try and maneuver your way into Griff's alliance. To see what he's planning."

She sat forward, tossing her long ebony hair over her shoulder. She leaned an elbow on her knee. "You know it's dangerous."

I nodded. "Yes, I do." I cocked a brow at her. "I have a sense that you have power over his type of creature."

"How do you know that?"

"You are one of the oldest creatures on this earth. Even older than him. Time must come with some sort of knowledge of dragons."

She smiled. "I can't change his mind if that's what you are implying."

"No, but you can convince him that you've turned on us."

She cocked her head. "Possibly." Her smile intensified. "You want me to keep an eye on Mariwen as well, don't you?"

"Yes." I leaned back, hoping I was doing the right thing and not putting Vanity in the way of danger.

Eloise popped in and interrupted us. "Maxi, I can look after her." She sat beside me on the bed and hung her head.

"I know you can, but if we get any Intel it will be as if Mari told us. And that puts her in danger." Saul had kept quiet through all this. I turned to him. "What do you think?"

He brushed a hand through his beard then toyed with his mustache. "It's dangerous, but I think it could work. The question is...," he turned to Vanity, "do you want to do it?"

She leaned back in the chair, stretching her long, lean body. "Well, it might liven this house up. Besides, I've never feared danger."

"Good, then it's settled. Saul, do you have any ideas on how to get started?"

His eyes crinkled in delight. "As a matter of fact, I've got an idea. The only way to make Griff realize Vanity has turned on us is for me to start a fight with her. You back me up, and if I know any dragon he will want to pull her to his side for numbers against us."

"It's a plan." She stood and stalked to the door. "Mind if I make the fight a little bloody?"

He grinned wide. "As long as you don't make it too deep."

"Sure thing, sugar."

She walked out the door and slammed it. Saul and I followed her out. She glided down the steps two at a time. "Damn it, Saul, you horrible little vermin," she screamed at him, causing the sound to echo through the house."

"Is that so?" he hollered, stomping after her.

She walked to the kitchen and stood, holding onto the island. "You are a despicable little gnome."

His face lit up and his smile spread across his face. "I'm a gnome, after all. It's what we are made of."

"Yes, but you lied to me...you made me think you had my back."

Griff, Mari, and Sally walked in and stood back as the scene unfolded.

"Vanity, gnomes lie...it's in our genetic makeup." He took off his hat and bowed. "It's been my utmost pleasure to dupe an elf of your standing."

She got close to him and peered into his face. "Well, you are finished duping me. I shall tell Griff everything you and Maxim have planned." Her face took on an eerie glow. "Everything." She enunciated every syllable, then hauled off and sucker punched him, causing him to flip upside down. Once he regained his composure he glared at her, wiping away the blood that trickled from his nose to his beard.

"Look Vanity, we never duped you. Saul is an upstanding gnome."

She threw her head back in laughter. "He's a damn gnome. They are not to be trusted."

I pretended to grow angry. "Fine, then go with the huge reptile if you want. You know he'll screw you too." I stalked off with Saul in tow. "Do you think he bought it?" I said under my breath.

"He had to...our acting was off the chain."

"Good. Now to ensure our win in this next master of domain competition."

"Then we must get plenty of sleep."

I opened the door to my room as Saul went to his next door. Sitting on my bed was Eloise, petting Zora, who purred in contentment.

"How did the fight go?" Zora asked.

"How do you know about that?"

"I told her," Eloise said in a mild tone, apparently still upset I wouldn't let her help us.

"We hope it worked," I replied, sitting on the bed.

Eloise crawled over to me and sat beside me. Her soft little hand touched mine. The feeling was surreal, as I could barely feel her.

"Are you mad at me?" she asked.

I looked at her and saw her eyes brimming with tears at the fear of my answer. "No, I'm just tired. It's been a long day."

Zora stood and stretched her body along the bed. "Come on, let's let Maxim rest. He's got a big day tomorrow." She weaved in and around us, her tail brushing against my arm, then leapt off the bed, her feet barely making a sound as she hit the hardwood floor. "Night."

As soon as they left and my head hit the pillow, sleep invaded me.

Nine

The next morning I woke from a calm sleep to me being thrown from my mattress... I peeked one eye open to see Eloise jumping on the bed again. She giggled and pointed at my prone body heaped on the floor next to the bed.

"Are you finally awake, Maxi?" she squealed out.

I pulled myself into a sitting position. "How long have you been here doing that?"

"Forever. I thought you were never going to wake. You were taking forever, and I thought you may be dead." She sighed in sadness. "But I never saw your ghost." She giggled again.

I rubbed my eyes, trying desperately to wake. From my peripheral vision, I saw a tray on the bedside table. "Who brought that?"

She rocked back and forth, twirling one pigtail. "Mari did."

I scooted back into bed propping myself against the headboard. "Does Griff know?"

She shook her head. "I don't think so, but Mari looked sad." She replied in her singsong voice.

I glanced over the tray and saw a folded-up note tucked underneath the plate. Quickly I scooped up the note and unfolded it.

Max,

Please meet me before the competition. Eloise says she knows of a secret place within the walls of the house. Thank you for looking after me in such a short time.

Mari

I folded it back and slid it underneath my pillow. Turning to Ely, I smiled and cocked my head. I brushed my long hair to the side to get a better look at the little girl. "Where is this secret tunnel you told Mari about?"

She kept brushing back the hair on her doll, never once looking at me. "You know the god-awful piece on the wall in the great room?" She made a face of dissatisfaction at the ornamental wall decoration. "The one with the ugly skulls on it? If you pull on the spikes on the bottom it opens a door. My daddy built it during the war. Lots of people escaped through it. It also has a room you can sit in and read, off to the right, just in case people figured out what Daddy was doing."

"Thank you, Eloise." I hugged her but fell face first on the bed.

She giggled. "Maxi, you need to warn me before you try to touch me. I must concentrate in order not to just go through you."

I stifled a laugh as I pushed myself back up. "I just thought, because you touched Zora...."

"Yes, but I'd been concentrating," she laughed. "Hurry and eat so I can show you how to get into the room."

I sat on the edge of the bed and took a few bites. Nerves got the better of me, and the want to see Mari prevailed. I stuffed a few more bites in, then looked at the clock. "Ely, we need to get going. Only an hour till the competition."

She stopped playing with her doll and placed it gently on the bed, then grabbed my hand. "Let's go. We should be careful Griff doesn't see us." I followed her downstairs. She stopped at the bottom and looked to the left, then to the right. She grabbed my hand tighter. "Hurry."

We ran across the room and stopped in front of the wall. She let go of my hand and ran her fingers across the spikes and counted. On the third one, she pulled it. It became longer than the others. She counted again, and on the seventh one, she pulled it too. A creaking sounded along the wall, and a portion of the wall slid forward.

"Go inside, she's waiting. I'll keep watch out here."

I slid between the two partitions of the wall and followed what had once been an underground railroad. Off to the left of the tunnel was a little room. A lone candle illuminated the small room. Mari stood with her back to me, her wings wrapped around her petite frame. Her long blonde hair cascaded down her back.

"Mari...."

She turned around and faced me. "Max, oh thank goodness you came. Griff has gotten worse...he's so full of anger. I wish my family hadn't gone to him."

I tipped her head back so she could look at me. "Then what about your brother?"

She thought and then started to cry. "I'd do anything for him."

I pulled her to me, and she sniffed against my chest. "Don't cry, Mari. I will do everything I can to get you out of your present situation."

She pulled back and wiped the tears away. "No, I'm afraid he will never stop. He will cheat and win."

"Then we'll come devise another plan. I promise."

She sighed. I pulled her closer and took the liberty of placing a tender kiss on her lips. She tasted like fresh strawberries and mint. "Mmm."

She pulled back and smiled. "What?"

"You taste like strawberries and mint."

She laughed. "It's my lip balm. Before I left, the princess came to me and gave me this." She held up a small tube. "A fairy's lips are sensitive when we are out of the realm. We are not used to the humidity. Though it doesn't bother us unless we are not protected by our magic for a long time. I liked how soft it made my lips, so I use it every day."

I cocked my head. "Louisiana is known for its humidity."

"Yes, but not the fairy realm. It's much cooler there. My home is different."

"Mari, will you come see me here after the competition? Make this our spot. If we have to leave together we can do so through here."

She nodded and fluttered up to face me. "I'll do anything I can to steal small moments with you."

"I'll have Eloise deliver a note when to meet me." We walked out of the room to see Eloise grinning at us. "What are you grinning about?" I asked her.

"Oh, nothing. Just so you know that room has a spell on it."

"What do you mean?" I asked.

"The room and the tunnel can only be seen by those who are in it." She grinned. "How do you think my father was able to get so many people through it?" She lowered her voice. "Except for the keeper of the dead."

"You mean Baron—"

She interrupted me. "Shhh, he'll hear you."

We stepped out of the secret passage to a barrage of voices. "Hurry, move away from the door and get by the seats," I instructed Mari. I pretended to check out the room while the others came in.

Ten

The skeletal man glided into the room, waving his hands around. "Gather around, ladies and gentlemen," Baron spoke through a cloud of dancing skeleton smoke. "Maxim's reign as master of domain has come to an end. So tonight, we will battle again." He turned to me. "You can also compete and try to win again."

I nodded. Saul came and stood beside me. "We have to win this."

"I agree." I glanced over to Mari, who stood beside Griff, his arm draped around her shoulders. Poor thing looked uncomfortable. She dropped her head and didn't look me in the face.

The loa of the dead clapped his hands together. "Let's head outside." We exited the house, and before us stood six platforms covered in spikes moving up and down. When the spikes had disappeared into the dais, Baron spoke.

"Please step onto your designated stage. You must balance yourselves on the spikes. If you fall you have lost."

Each platform had one of our names at the bottom. We all stepped forward and stood upon our stands. Then the ground below us opened, filling with murky water. In seconds a swamp surrounded us. As I watched the water rise, so did the spikes. We all balanced on the spikes, careful not to fall.

"Now," Baron laughed, "the last person standing will become the next master of domain."

The spikes bobbed spontaneously, trying to knock us off balance. Then the fun began, as the platforms moved in different directions. I tried to keep my balance when a dozen or so silver objects flew at me. One caught me and grazed me on the side. I almost fell off but regained my balance. I couldn't take my attention away from my predicament but I sensed the others were dealing with their own devices now, and all I could do was remain standing. Down below us swam an alligator, snapping its jaws, hoping for a meal. Every time I tried to check on Mari another round of silver flew in my direction. Over to the right, I saw stepping stones emerge from the water, only to disappear underneath again. I wondered what purpose they served.

To my right I saw the dragon standing as still as a statue, moving in sync to the motions of his stage. From my position, I couldn't tell if he was cheating. In front of him floated a huge mirror, but he gazed into it without emotion.

As I refocused, a scream echoed through the air. I spun my head around and saw Mari fall from her platform into the water. The gator, which had swum away, turned and made its way to her. Without thinking of the consequences, I jumped from one stepping stone to the next.

"No, Maxim!" Saul screamed out.

From the corner of my eye, I saw him jumping up and down, flailing his hands, willing me to stop. At the edge of the last stepping stone, I stopped. Then without hesitation, I dove underwater as the gator swam faster, using his tail as a rudder. Reaching her just in time, I grabbed her under her arms and swam as fast as I could as the gator gained on me. No way in hell was I going to let her be dinner for this swamp reptile.

Quickly, I pushed a drenched Mari onto the levee and pulled myself alongside her. The alligator stopped at the levee embankment, turned around, and swam back toward the others, hoping for a meal to fall into his jaws. I leaned closer to Mari and noticed that her breathing was labored.

"Are you all right?" I questioned, fearing the worst. I smoothed away her wet hair from her face. She looked pale, and for a second I thought she was dead.

The others remained on their platforms, and now my fate rested in Saul's abilities to win for all of us. Somehow I figured this was all Griff's doing. I scooped her up into my arms and carried her inside. Her shallow breathing worried me, but I wasn't going to let her die on my watch. I hated Griff so much for trying to hurt Mari to get to me. She was a means to an end, nothing more.

I leaned down and nuzzled Mari's face, and kissed her on the forehead as I carried her inside. "Please be okay," I pleaded.

She stirred as I placed her on the sofa. Her breathing became more normal as she lay there. Her eyelashes lay wet against her eyelids as I stared into her face and willed her to open her eyes. They started to flutter open and my heart beat faster. I stroked her face and the soft skin burned my hand. She was burning with fever.

"Oh shit, what were we going to do now?"

Eloise popped in, singing, but stopped when she saw us there. "What happened, Maxi?" She ran over to us.

"She fell into the water during the comp." I choked back tears. "Eloise, she can't die." I held back a string of tears that was threatening to emerge.

"She's not going to die. She's a fairy."

Then I thought about it. "Her poison is iron. Perhaps some iron entered her body as the silver did mine." I layed my head beside her body on the sofa. Heat radiated from her body. I sniffed back a tear. When I'd auditioned for the reality show, never in a million years had I thought I'd find my one true love.

Eloise patted me on the back. "She'll be fine, we just need to find the iron and remove it." Just then Saul entered the house, the explicit words coming out of his mouth causing Eloise to blush. She eyed me and whispered, "Maxi, he's saying bad words."

"I know. Not a good sign, especially since he's in the house and Griff is still out there." Saul stalked over, his expression grim. "What happened—?" I started to ask.

He interrupted me, not answering my question. "How's she doing?"

I looked at him holding back worry and anger. "The iron must have penetrated her body. Her breathing has returned to normal, but she has a fever."

He nodded. "Good, we need to get her healed."

"How? She's the healer here."

"Not the only one." Vanity walked inside. "Shhh, we need to hurry before Griff comes inside."

I hung my head. "He's going to win," I muttered.

Vanity's eyes softened but told me the truth. Griff had won the second Mari fell into the water.

"Let me help you. I may be able to pull the toxins from her."

"How? Why didn't you let us in on this little secret of yours?" I asked her.

"Because you didn't ask?" She grinned.

"But when I was ill—"

She stopped me with a wave of her hand. "Do you want to continue to fight with me, or do you want me to help her?"

I nodded. "This is not over."

Mari stirred and grabbed my hand. "Griff did this to me." Her voice was raspy and low, her lips dry and caked.

"How?" I asked. I pulled out some lip balm from my pocket.

"Let me do my magic, please." Vanity ushered me out of the way.

"Wait." I pulled off the cap and gently moistened my lips, then kissed her softly. When I was done, I handed the tube to Vanity. "Here, she'll need this when she wakes."

"Come on, Maxim." Saul helped me up. "Let's go outside and get some air."

Hesitantly I followed him, but before going outside I looked over my shoulder at the elf and fairy. The moment I stepped outside my anger fueled as Griff hopped off his platform.

"Congratulations, Griff. You have won master of domain for the week."

His face was etched with satisfaction. I stomped over to him.

"Why did you do this to her?"

He looked abashed. "What in the hell do you mean?"

"Mari said you are the cause of her being hurt."

He grinned devilishly. "It was a means to the end. I knew if I got her off the platform you would stop the world to save her." He inched closer to me, his breath hot. "You damn alpha werewolves, always wanting to save every fucking thing."

"So this is how you cheated." Saul walked up and kicked him in the shin.

Griff became angered and in seconds Saul dangled by two fingers of the dragon, and his feet dangled in the air. "Look, you little weed, you kick me one more time and you will find yourself gator food." He spun him around and dangled him over the swamp, which had now begun to drain.

Saul crossed his arms over his chest, showing no sign of fear. "Let me go now!" he yelled and swung himself back and forth. Then the dragon screamed in agony as Saul clamped his teeth on Griff's forearm.

"Why, you little imp." He dropped him.

Saul kicked him in the shin again, straightened his hat, and twirled his mustache. "I'm a garden gnome, not an imp, you oversized reptile."

Thunder cracked in the sky and we stopped. The torrential rain poured, causing us to run inside before we became drenched. "Come on,

Saul, let's go check on Mari." I hollered over the loudness.

Griff stepped in front of me. "No, she's mine."

I glared at him. "You didn't even help her when she fell off. In fact," I paused, "what did you do, push her off?"

He grinned and licked his lips. "Well, to be honest, yes. Thanks to your heroic behavior, you've helped me win." He slapped me on the back. "Thanks, I'll take it from here. I'm sure Vanity has her healed enough by now." He walked away from us.

"Son of a bitch. Vanity lied to us...he sent her in there," Saul muttered under his breath.

I shook my head. "No, it can't be. She must be pretending like we asked her to." I tried to convince not only him but myself. I walked toward the house, my feet heavy as I trudged forward. How in the hell was I going to remain in here to protect Mari? As we entered the house, I glanced over and saw Baron Samedi smiling at us.

"I shall return momentarily to congratulate Griff on his winning." He waved at us while puffing on his cigar. Then he tipped his hat and turned away, walking off.

Eleven

I glanced around for Mari and watched as Griff scooped her up, but before our eyes, she was taken and placed back on the sofa.

"What the hell!" he exclaimed. He kept trying, but she wouldn't budge. He turned to me. "Are you doing this?"

"How in the hell could I? I'm nowhere near her," I fired back.

He unsuccessfully continued to try to pick her up and growled loudly. "Vanity, when you get a chance can you try to move Mariwen from the sofa?" His tone was full of sarcasm. He stalked away with Sally glued to him.

Saul walked inside and stalked up to Vanity. He pointed a finger at her. "You stabbed us in the back."

With her hands on her hips, she glared at him. "How? I saved her."

"You didn't tell us it was on behalf of him," he said gruffly.

"Look, you asked me to get close to him, so I did."

I stepped between the two and looked at Saul. I shook my head. "She has a point." I glanced back to the elf. "Sorry. We are just a bit on edge, knowing that he's won."

"He was banking on that. He knew you would save her."

"Did you get all the poison out of her?" I whispered to her.

She nodded her head. "I think so, but she will need plenty of rest."

"You think so?" Saul inclined his head.

"It's hard to say since she fell into the water. We'll have to wait and see. I'll keep an eye on her."

I sighed and ran a hand through my hair. "Damn it, I just wish it was me being able to comfort her."

"Maxim, rest assured he won't be comforting her. He doesn't have it in his nature to be that kind to anyone," Vanity reassured me.

"I know, but I want to be there with her instead of it being him."

She patted my arm. "I know, but I'll be there to keep an eye on her. Have comfort in that."

"I will thanks." I hugged her and whispered, "Saul didn't mean what he said. He won't admit it, but I think he's got a soft spot for Mari."

She smiled. "I know. I'd better get back before he thinks I'm playing both sides." She scooped the fairy up in her arms, and this time the house let her remove her from the sofa.

Saul and I trudged up the steps. "You know we'll have to serve that damned Griff."

His expression took on an almost evil glint. "I wonder what his poison is."

"Why?" I inquired.

He shrugged. "Oh, I don't know, but if I must serve him food, I may add a secret ingredient."

I stopped him. "No, because if he finds out he'll kill you."

"Ahh Maxim, do you have a soft spot for this ole garden gnome?" he joked.

"It's just in such a short time we've known each other, I consider you my friend."

He jumped up on my shoulder and patted my head. "You know I consider you a friend. I got your back. Now let's go rest before we have to serve that giant ass scaly reptile."

As we trudged upstairs, I pondered the possibility of me leaving the house. A tiny hand grabbed mine and I looked at Eloise. "Mr. Maxi, is Miss Mari going to be okay?" she questioned, glistening tears slid down her face.

I stopped at the top step, knelt, and wiped the tear from her face. The teardrop balanced on my hand. No doubt magic at work here.

"Yes, Eloise, but will you do me a small favor?"

She nodded her head vigorously. "Anything for you."

"Good. Can you tell me more about this house and its magic?"

"Sure."

She grabbed my hand and Saul's and headed to my room. Once we were in my room she let go of our hands, then jumped up on the bed and sat at the head of it on a mountain of pillows. Saul curled up in a chair across from her and combed his beard with his hand. The silver jewelry adoring his hand shone in the light of the room. I sat at the small table in the room.

"All right, Eloise, we're listening."

"Good. My daddy was the most powerful witch in New Orleans. He was the leader of the Cypress Coven, a coven which has been around forever. In fact, it still exists today. Anyway, he built this house, and in every board and every nail infused his own magic inside. So, if he were to ever pass he would still be around. Even if the house were to be burned down it would magically repair itself. My father had the ability to invoke all the elements. No one else has ever been able to do that, except one other witch in this time. Not even me."

"Can it help us stop Griff from cheating?"

She shook her head. "No, I'm afraid not. Because when he cheats its outside, which isn't under the house's protection."

"Well damn." I sighed deeply, then glanced at Eloise. Quickly an idea popped into my head.

"I know the house is magic, but...can it keep Mari safe?"

"Oh yes, it keeps all good souls safe. She's a fairy, so hers is one of the purest. My father was a good witch, a kind man, and so are all his descendants. This house has its own soul, magically created by my father."

"Good. I think we can create a little havoc in the house." I thought to myself, *even if I leave Mari will be okay.* "Ely, do you think you can get the house to start messing with him?"

She nodded. "I suspect the house has already been messing with him since his soul is dark."

"How?" I questioned.

She laughed. "Don't you remember Griff trying to leave with Mari? That was the house working against him." She smiled as she glanced around the room.

"Ely, how did you die?"

She stared back at me with wide eyes. "A very bad man who hated my father tried to get to him. My father spelled the house so that it protected us, so the bad man waited and hoped he would leave. But he didn't leave...instead, it was me. I'd left my dolly outside. I thought if I hurried no danger would happen to me." She held it in her hands as she told the story. "My mother followed me outside and the demon killed us both. I never saw it happen, it was just over. In the next second I was back in the house, but my mommy wasn't. Later I heard that Daddy had made a deal with the loa of the dead."

I gasped. "Is that how Baron Samedi has the house?"

She grinned. "Yes, but on one condition. He got to take one of us to the underworld and one stayed here. My daddy chose me since my mother pleaded with him to let her go."

"Doesn't it get lonely here for you?"

Her smile curved her lips upward and her eyes shimmered. She shook her head. "My daddy is here everywhere. When he finally died his body and soul merged into the house. Besides, I can leave the house and go into the garden."

I cocked my head. "Garden?"

She laughed again. "Silly. Where you have your competitions. You see the underworld, I see the garden my mother worked on with all the pretty flowers. I see her in every petal and every leaf. See, both my parents are here with me always. It's how our coven works." Her expression grew grim.

"What's wrong?" Saul asked, finally speaking while wiping a tear from his face. When he caught me looking he growled, "What?" He pretended the story hadn't affected him.

I grinned. "Do you need a tissue?" I joked with him.

"No. Eloise, finish your story please." He scowled at me.

"Baron Samedi requested one other thing...that I couldn't keep my witch powers."

A question popped into my head. "So, does your coven still exist?"

She nodded her head and grinned wide. "Well, sort of...I left out the best part. I had an older sister and brother. They had left years ago but returned after our deaths. My sister created the Crescent coven, and it became the matriarch witch coven. Then my brother, who took over our coven, made it stronger. Down through the years, the Crescent coven was controlled by the women in my family, and the Cypress by the men. Eventually, my brother appointed the Delacroix family, known for their powerful nature to the elements. Both covens have strengthened, and today they have become even more powerful than imagined, by marriage twice."

"Do the witches know about the house?"

She tilted her head. "Yes, but they have their own lives and wish not to live here. They have also made deals with the loa. This is my house."

The lights flickered in the room and Eloise laughed.

A knock resounded on the door. "Come in."

Vanity peeked inside. "Just wanted to let you know Mari is fine."

"Thank goodness," I sighed but mumbled under my breath. "Damn, I want to end Griff." A surge of power flowed through me. Saul glanced over at me and cocked an eyebrow at me.

"If you keep this up you'll certainly become alpha," he chuckled.

"Ahem." Vanity cleared her throat. "Another thing, Griff wants you and Saul to cook his dinner."

I groaned loudly. "Geeze. Come on, Saul, let's get this over with."

We shuffled out of the room and down the stairs. "What are we going to cook the oversized reptile?" Saul asked.

"No idea. What the hell does a dragon eat?" I laughed.

"People?" he offered.

I shook my head. "We can't." We entered the kitchen and saw Mari standing in front of the stove. "Mari." I softly spoke her name. She turned around, a weak smile covered her face. In three strides, I made it to her, and without thinking held her in my arms. "Are you okay?"

She leaned into me but quickly pushed away. "I'm okay. I'm a quick healer." She smiled and held me at arm's length. "Be careful, Griff has Sally keeping an eye on me." She turned her attention to the stove. "I figured you and Saul would need help here." She waved her hand over the meal.

"How'd you convince him to let you help us?"

She shrugged. "I didn't ask him." She turned to Saul. "Also, I needed to make sure y'all didn't try and poison him."

"How'd you know?" He looked shocked.

"Because trust me, I've thought of it as well. Besides "It figures the dragon would have an ace up his sleeve."

She scooped the food onto a plate and placed it on a tray. "Now hurry. After he eats, we will have the nomination ceremony." She hastily left the room just as Sally entered.

She glowered at us. "Is Griff's food ready?"

I grumbled. "Yes, we're coming."

"Good." She replied empathically tossing her hair over her shoulder.

I grabbed the tray and nodded for Saul to come with me. He jumped off the counter and followed me out, grumbling the entire time.

Twelve

We entered the room where Griff sat atop a throne covered in dragon scales. I glanced around, and everyone was there except Mari. Vanity eyed me and mouthed, "She's in her room resting."

I refocused my attention on the dragon and glowered at him. Keeping my attention on Griff, I bent down and under my breath asked, "Saul, did I look like a pompous asshole when I sat on my throne?"

He shook his head. "Not one bit. You, my friend, are humble," he whispered from the side of his mouth.

We walked forward and I bowed. "Your food, Griff." I offered the tray to him, placing it on his lap.

"It's about time," he barked loudly.

Baron Samedi entered the house, followed by skeleton filled smoke. "Hello everyone, how are we today?" he asked, grinning. "Are we ready for the selection ceremony today?"

"After I finish eating," Griff spoke as he placed the fork into his mouth.

"No, now!" Baron Samedi narrowed his eyes at the dragon. The tray disappeared in a puff of smoke. I stifled a laugh, not knowing if it was the loa or the house that caused it to disappear.

"But...," he spat. Griff looked pissed but soon changed his expression when the loa glared at him.

Baron Samedi stalked up the steps to Griff's throne. "Don't let the power get to your head where I'm concerned. I'm still loa of the dead, and I can end you before your times over in the house." He turned to the rest of us and clapped his hands. "Let's begin now. Griff, please go to your room and gather the coffin and voodoo dolls for who you wish to nominate today."

Griff begrudgingly stomped down the steps. We waited patiently for him to return. The skeleton loa leaned against the throne, puffing on his cigar. Tiny dancing skeletons gyrated around the room. Within seconds Griff was back and placed the chest on the marble table. He opened the lid, and when he turned around an expression of satisfaction etched across his face. He placed his hands behind his back and smugly smiled at me.

"Who have you nominated?" Baron Samedi asked.

He scooped the first doll out. "Maxim, you are my first choice," he sneered, "and my target." He placed it on the table. It stood magically upright. "Next I choose Saul." The other voodoo doll stood beside mine. They danced together behind Griff's back, I sensed the house was behind this action.

"Thank you, Griff," the loa said, then focused on me, smiling. "This concludes our ceremony." I held back my anger, unlike Griff had when I nominated him. My only recourse now was to win the immunity. Griff grinned like a loon as he stalked off, celebrating his nominations. I walked out of the room and into the living room.

Eloise suddenly appeared. "I'm sorry, Mr. Maxi. Don't worry, you'll win the immunity."

My doubt enveloped me. "I don't know, Ely. Can you do me a favor and get a message to Mari, asking her to meet me in our spot?"

"I'm on it." She donned a detective hat as she smiled at me.

I laughed. "Where did you get that?"

She giggled. "I'm a detective off to give Miss Mari the clue." She disappeared with a pop.

I walked silently into the great room and glanced around, making sure no one was lurking. Sitting on the bench, I waited.

"How are you?" Zora purred at me.

"Holy crap." I jumped. "You scared the shit out of me."

She cocked her head. "Sorry, Max." She sat and licked her paws. "How's it going?"

I shrugged. "Eh, you know. I just got nominated by Griff."

She continued to lick her paw. "Well, that was inevitable. The dragon has had it out for you since you walked into the house."

"How did you...?" I paused, remembering she was a magical creature privy to all that was paranormal. I dropped my head and sighed. "I know."

"Maxim, what happened to your reason of why you came into the house?" she asked.

I shook my head. "I don't know, Zora. I never wanted this. Though every day the alpha part of me is trying to break free. I want to protect Mari at all costs, even if it means not becoming human." As the words flowed, I came to a conclusion of what I must do. I had to speak to Mari first.

The cat rubbed against my leg. "Should I send word to your father then?"

I petted her. "No, I need to do this on my own."

She smiled. "Spoken like a true alpha."

Mari walked in, interrupting us. "Max, what's up?"

I stood, rushed to her, and held her. Then I leaned in and made a bold movement...I kissed her like I'd never done before. As I pulled back, still inches from her lips, I spoke. "Mari, let's run away."

Her eyes glinted. "Really? Wait what about my family, my brother?"

"Shhh." I quieted her with my finger to her lips. "Let's discuss this inside there." I inclined my head to our secret place. We walked hand in hand to the wall. I opened it the way I'd seen Eloise do and the wall opened. As we stepped inside we were met by Baron Samedi. "Shit!" I exclaimed. "How'd he find out?" I murmured to Mari.

"Because I know all that goes on in this house. Besides, there are cameras hidden all around the house, as you know." He leaned against the dingy bricks lining the tunnel, puffing on a cigar. Mari held my hand tighter. The skeleton man walked toward us. "Maxim and Mariwen, I'm sorry to say you can't leave. You signed up for this, and must let the game play out."

"But...I...didn't...," Mari protested.

He shook his head. "That I'm sorry about, but once you stepped foot inside your fate was written."

Anger swarmed around me. "This isn't fair. She doesn't want this."

Baron Samedi's face took on an evil glint. His mouth opened, and in the void, I saw death and destruction. "Do not speak to me in such a manner, wolf. I will not tolerate such insolence."

I backed away, not because he scared me, but more for Mari. If he'd ended me then I wouldn't be around to protect her. "Fine," I grumbled loudly.

He nodded and stuck his cigar back into the corner of his mouth. "Now please go back inside the house. We will be starting the immunity challenge perhaps tomorrow. Both of you go get some rest."

He waited for us to turn around and head back out where we had come from, then followed us back through the wall. We slipped out quickly and the trap door closed behind us. We walked out and sat on the bench.

He turned to Mari. "Please don't think of trying to leave once my back is turned."

As he left the both of us sat in silence, trying to figure a way to get out of there.

Thirteen

The next afternoon Saul and I walked into the great hall and waited. Baron popped in and strutted through the house. Soon all the others joined us. He looked at Mari as she entered the room. "I'm sorry, but I can't allow you to play this one. You are still recovering."

"But...."

He shook his head. "The house decides your fate...please go rest."

She looked back at me as she left the room. "Be careful, Max, and win this."

I was deep in thought when Saul sat beside me. "What's going on in that head of yours?"

I shrugged. "Nothing really, trying to focus on this next comp."

He slapped me on the back. "Good, we need to win this."

Baron Samedi stood facing us. "Are we ready to play?" He smiled eerily. "Let's go outside." We all followed him to the door, but before I stepped outside he stopped me. "I'm rooting for you, wolf." Then he exited the house.

We walked outside to a huge void. Suddenly before us, a scene formed. Huge cypress trees emerged from the dank and murky bayou to the left of us. I sucked in a breath in awe as they became huge, with branches and moss hanging from them. The wind blew and curly tendrils of Spanish moss reached out to us.

"Gather around for our second immunity challenge." Baron Samedi waved his hands. Huge stalks of sugarcane sprouted from the ground, forming a maze. Before us within the cane stalks five doors appeared. "You all have a key. It opens your door to the maze." Keys floated down and dropped at our feet. I picked up mine and held it tight in my hand. "Once inside you must find other keys to open the cypress boxes placed in different places throughout the maze. But be careful. Some will contain a gas that will render the one who opened it unconscious, though some will contain your next key. Once a box is opened it remains that way. The first to find the key for immunity will be the winner."

Saul bumped my leg. "We've got this. No way he can cheat at this.

"Don't be so sure." Somehow doubt filled my soul. He would do anything to get me out of the house and away from Mari. "We have to do our best."

The air swirled around us, then calmed. "All right, are y'all ready to start?" Baron Samedi asked.

We all nodded in unison. I glanced over at Griff, who glared at me smugly.

"You can enter the maze now," Baron instructed us.

We all ran for our doors. I stuffed the key into the lock and turned. When it clicked, I pushed the door made of sugar cane stalks open. It caught on the ground below, so I pushed harder. Finally, it scraped open. Before me on either side stood huge tight cane stalks. I ran through the tunnel, wondering where Saul was.

Before I could wander further, a rustling noise scratched from one of the maze walls. I peeked in and saw him struggling to get over to me. When he pushed through, he tumbled out and landed head over ass on the ground in front of me. His hat flew a couple of feet in front of him, revealing a nice neat Mohawk. He dusted himself off, grabbed his hat, and straightened it back on his head.

I chuckled. "You all right?"

He nodded, finished dusting off his pants, then looked at me. He twirled his mustache and grinned. "You ready to win this?"

"Sure, where do we start?"

"Not sure, but let's get started."

After a few left and right turns, we came across a box. My heart stopped. "Wait, we don't have a key."

Saul looked around. "It has to be around here somewhere." He began hunting through the maze walls of stalks. He delved deeper into the wall. "Max, I think I found it." I peered through the waving stalks of sugar cane, not seeing much of anything. Then I saw it lingering high, shimmering in the darkness, hanging onto something on a stalk. Saul was already climbing his way to it.

He came back out, dirt on his face and hat. He even had a cane leaf stuck in his hat. I pulled it out and dropped it to the ground. As I took the key he offered me I stopped. "Why are you helping me?"

He eyed me. "Because you're my friend, and I don't like Griff. Besides, I owe the cat." He mumbled the last part.

"What was that?" I grinned.

"I owe that cat."

"For what?" I asked.

"Look, we can talk about that later. Check the damn key."

"All right, but this is not over." I eyed him with suspicion.

My palm sweated holding the key, but as I pushed it into the lock, I held my breath. Turning it, I heard the click. I slowly opened it and revealed a shiny silver key.

"Grab it and let's go," he hollered as he ran to his left.

I did as instructed and followed him. Up ahead we saw a body sprawled out on the dirt. We ran over to it and realized that Sally had inhaled a toxic gas. The box remained opened and her key lay on the ground, so I grabbed it.

"Hurry Saul, she'll be fine once it wears off."

After two more keys and thankfully no gas, rounding the next two corners I saw a box gleaming in the moonlight. "Saul, there it is...it must be."

"Then run for it, hurry."

I did, my hand reached out for it. Once it was firmly in my grasp, I held it close to my chest, breathing a sigh of relief that I'd found it. Then I placed it back down as Saul came to stand beside me.

"Do you think that's the right one?" he asked.

"It has to be." My hands shook as I stuck the key in the lock. It clicked open and I sniffed.

"What are you doing?" Saul inquired.

"Trying to see if I can sense any danger."

He shook his head. "Hurry and open it," he laughed.

Gently I lifted the lid. No gas came out, so I pushed the lid further back. Inside sat a small marble encrusted key.

"You did it," Saul exclaimed.

I nodded. "But that means you're leaving."

He patted me on the back. "Yes, but I'll always be looking after you."

Behind me, laughter echoed.

"Too late, wolf, it's mine." I stood up and held the key tight. Griff grinned wide, and something tugged at the key in my hand. He held an object in his hand that lit up the night sky. The box lifted from my arms and flew to Griff.

"Damn it, Griff. It's mine...I won it fair and square," I yelled, and lunged at him. As he fell back to the ground, I stood over him and growled.

He just lay there and laughed, then pushed me off him. As I flew backward and skidded in the dirt, I watched him right himself and chuckle.

"What the hell is so funny?"

He stood and dusted his slacks off in disgust. "The key is mine, or Mari and her family are dead," he snickered.

Saul came over and kicked him hard in the shins. "Maxim won that key fair. It's his."

The dragon grinned at him. "Fine, here, take it, but your precious fairy will be dead by the fortnight."

I glanced at Saul, who expressed sadness in knowing what I would be doing. I realized Griff had no mind to cheat...this time he was just going to steal. As I handed him back the key, I asked. "Why do you want to become human?"

"I don't."

"Well then, why are you here?"

"That is none of your business. But if you must know, I want to rid the world of fairies."

"What about Mari?"

He threw his head back and laughed. "Yes, her too, but only after I've turned the entire fairy world human."

I growled low in my belly. "You've never cared for her."

He shook his head.

"Why?"

He shrugged his shoulders. "It's a long-standing feud I've had with those little good-doers." He walked around, then turned back to face us. "It's why I was so surprised to have the fairies contact me to help them. They must not have known." He tsked. "King Roi will certainly be upset." He twirled the key around his finger. "His world is crumbling around him, and yet he'll never be able to fix it. I must get back to the loa of the dead and let him know 'I' won." He laughed out loud, sending chills along my spine.

As he walked away, I turned to Saul. "We need to let Mari know what Griff has planned. She doesn't realize he knows all the fairies' secrets."

"Think we should let Baron Samedi know he stole it from you?"

I shook my head. "He said once we stepped inside the house our fate was in the hands of the game. He'll just see it as another part of this." I waved my hands around.

I shoved my hands in my pockets on the way back and thought of nothing but Mari.

Fourteen

Once we reached the others Griff was already celebrating his win, even if it was ill-gotten. I stalked past the party, followed by Saul. Hopefully, Griff would brag more, giving me time to let Mari in on Griff's plan.

We entered the house. Mari sat at the table drinking a glass of water, her skin much paler than when I'd last seen her. I rushed to her side. "Are you all right?" She nodded her head, but I sensed she lied. "Hold on, don't leave." I figured I could tell her later about Griff. I went to the great hall and called out softly, "Zora."

She padded in, her tail swishing back and forth. "You called?"

"Yes. Can you get back to Mari's realm for me?"

She sat on her haunches. "For what reason?"

"She's sick, and I fear she needs some fairy magic to heal her."

"But Max, she's a healer. She should be able to heal herself."

I nodded. "I know, but something is wrong and she's not healing."

She licked her paw, then combed her whiskers. "It may be dangerous for you without me here."

"I don't care."

She bobbed her head up and down. "Instead of her family, though, I'll contact the voodoo practitioner, Cassandra, for help. That way I'll keep her family out of danger."

"They are already in danger. Griff plans on turning them all human. That's why he's here."

Her eyes went wide. "We can't allow him to win."

I shook my head. "I may not have anything to do with that. You know he wants me out of the house."

"I know, which means I think our mission in the house has changed. Once you leave the house you must somehow get back inside."

I nodded. "I will."

"It will be difficult if I'm not here with you."

"Still, you must get to her family as soon as possible. The expulsion ceremony isn't for at least four more days. Make sure you are back here."

She cocked her head at me, then turned and left, swishing her tail back and forth.

Three days later

"Saul, I'm worried about Zora not returning in time before I leave here."

He sat back on the sofa in my room, his right leg crossed over the other as he groomed his beard. "I'd be more concerned about you leaving."

"What do you mean?"

"Not sure, but I've been getting an eerie vibe about the house, or actually outside of the house."

A soft knock on the door interrupted us. "Come in."

Mari peeked her head around the door and smiled weakly. I jumped off the bed and practically scooped her into my arms. "How are you doing?"

"Fine, I'm feeling stronger," she lied.

"You shouldn't be here. What if Griff finds out?"

She covered her mouth and giggled like a little girl. "He won't be waking for a while. I gave him a sedative when he demanded I make him lunch."

My hand went around her neck and I caressed it. "Mari, you need to be careful. He'll kill you if he finds out."

"He won't."

I carried her over to the bed. "Mari, what happens to fairies when they stay in the human world too long?"

She cocked her head and thought. "Well, the princess was out in the human world and she seemed fine when she returned home."

"What if they get sick out in the human world?" I asked instead.

She sighed. "I don't know, it's never happened." She fell against my shoulder, her body hot to the touch.

"Saul, can you try and get Vanity in here please?"

He nodded and bounded out of the room. Within a few minutes, the door cracked open and Vanity peered around the door.

"Come in." I ushered her inside. "Is there anything else you can do for her?"

"I can try. I fear Mari has been out of her realm too long." Sadness crept through her facial expressions. "Maxim, I should have realized that she would become sicker outside of her realm."

I couldn't be mad at her, I just wanted Mari better. "I wish Zora would hurry and return. I don't know what's taking her so long. She should have been back by now."

As Vanity placed her hands over Mari, I saw a hazy substance being pulled from her body and into Vanity's hands. "What's happening?" I asked.

"I'm pulling the poison from her body. I'll try this a little each day, though I can't promise it will work. It needs another body to be transferred to. One that is strong enough to hold it."

"Why couldn't you have done this before?"

"Because if I'd have pulled it from her before it would have surely killed her." She glanced at me. "An option I didn't think you would have liked."

I shook my head in agreement.

"Besides, I don't want Griff to get wind of what I can do."

Before she could utter another word, the door slammed open, bouncing off the wall and swinging back. In the door frame stood one angry dragon. "What the hell is going on here?" he demanded. In the blink of an eye, Vanity tossed what poison she had pulled from Mari at Griff. He never saw it coming as the invisible force catapulted him backward.

Mari sat, her color returning to a smidge of normalcy. Griff rebounded and roared at us. "Who did that?"

"I did," Mari spoke.

"You what?" he roared. "Why?"

She gained some confidence and stood, wobbling. "Because I'm tired of you being a bully. I came here to talk to Max. You don't own me yet." She squared her shoulders at him.

He harrumphed. "Fine, but this isn't over yet. I'm sending your little boyfriend out of the house."

I growled at him, feeling little hairs erupt on my forearms.

"Don't, Max."

"I can protect you."

She shook her head. "No, you can't."

"But...," I pleaded.

"Shhh. I'll go with him. Thanks for everything you've done for me." She trailed a finger down my chest. The touch lit me on fire. I wanted to grab her and head for the secret tunnel and take her from this horrid place. I sighed, knowing the only way out was to be sent out by votes. I shook my head. *What have I gotten myself into*? How could I have let my heart take over what I really wanted...to be human? Now I was doomed to lose the one thing I desperately wanted, which had changed since being in the house...now it was her. I watched her with a heavy heart as she walked away with Griff. I sighed deeply, realizing I hadn't been able to let her in on Griff's plans for her.

The door closed with a thud and I jumped at the sound. Saul walked over to me. "We need to figure out a way to get rid of him."

I sat and dropped my head into my hands. "Yes, but how? I have one more day here."

He sat beside me, his legs dangling over the bed. "I was going to leave if you left since my job would be done, but I'll stay to watch over her."

I looked up, tears threatening to slide down my face. "Thank you. You are a good friend."

He compassionately smiled something that I rarely saw from him. "We are friends for life. And when I get out of here I'll find you… I promise you I'll make sure that Mari stays safe.

"Good, thanks." I laid back on the bed and got comfortable, my thoughts all over the place. "I think I need some rest for tomorrow."

"All right, Max, I'll see you tomorrow." He left, closing the door silently. As I drifted off to sleep, I wondered where Zora could be.

Fifteen

Expulsion Ceremony

I woke late to the sound of music playing and trudged downstairs to the kitchen. Mari once again stood in front of the stove, her body moving to the tune that played throughout the house. I watched her for what seemed like an eternity. How could I leave her here?

She turned to me, and that smile I'd fallen in love with softened her face. "Hello, Max."

"Mari, you look better."

She blushed. "Do I?"

"Well yes," I lied, still seeing a hint of dark shadows under her eyes.

"Would you like something to eat?"

"Yes, but are you sure you should be cooking it? Won't Griff be upset?"

She inched closer to me. "It'll be our little secret," she flirted.

I smiled like I hadn't smiled in forever. "Sure, why not?"

I watched her as she busied herself cooking. I tried to open my mouth to tell her what Griff was planning, but for some reason, I couldn't. I just continued to watch her movements, wishing I could be with her forever.

She placed a plate in front of me and pulled me from my thoughts. "Here, eat."

My mouth was instantly dry, and I sipped some water to choke down the food. Once I was able to swallow, I smiled at Mari. "This is good."

"Thank you. I'd better get this to Griff before he sends Sally to look for me."

I stopped her as she went to leave. "Mari, please be safe and keep Saul close to you."

I held her hand, not wanting to let go. She put the tray down and leaned into me. When her lips touched mine, my soul burned inside. All my emotions came to the forefront, as did my alpha nature. I wanted to protect her...no, I had to protect her. The kiss intensified as I cupped the back of her neck and pulled her closer. She pulled back, and my heart tugged inside my chest. I wanted to say so much to her but couldn't will my mouth to open. She picked up the tray and left. I finished breakfast in silence, wishing I could experience that kiss forever.

Eloise popped in beside me, tugging on my pants leg. "Mr. Maxi, Zora still hasn't returned. I'm afraid something bad has happened to her."

I feared the same thing...I just didn't want to say it out loud. All I could do was nod.

She tugged on my pants leg again. In seconds, my anger came full force, running like a hurricane inside my body. As soon as Eloise touched my arm, my fury dissipated.

"I know you want to kill him," she comforted me. "But while you are in the house, you can't."

I growled low.

"What's all this growling about?" Saul shuffled into the room.

"Nothing, Mr. Saul. I was just reminding him he can't kill the stupid dragon in the house."

He laughed. "Then we will have to get him out of the house."

I sighed. "It's a little late for that, now isn't it?"

He cocked an eyebrow at me. "Yes, I suppose, but don't count me out. Or that fairy, for that matter."

"But I—"

He interrupted me. "Your alpha nature is emerging, isn't it?"

I nodded. "How'd you know?"

"Your alpha energy flows throughout the house. That's probably why Griff doesn't like you. He sensed it the moment you entered the house."

I hung my head. "I'm at such a loss not being able to help or control my fate."

Saul hopped onto the table and looked at me. "I don't care what that skeletal man told you. Only we control our fates, our destinies. Us!" He bellowed loudly.

"You are right, but I'm still leaving the house."

He nodded. "What you do outside of the house is yours and yours only."

A loud boom echoed around the house, signifying Baron Samedi's entrance. "Gather in the great hall, please."

I sighed loudly and shoved my dishes into the sink, then trudged off to meet with the others. They all sat on the benches, and I scooted in beside Vanity. Griff stood in front of us, sneering in my direction.

"Without further ado, let's get this ceremony started." Baron Samedi waved his hands over the small coffin containing the two voodoo dolls. A bowl of pins sat on it. "One by one you will each vote by placing a pin in the doll for the creature you want out."

Vanity stepped forward and walked to the table and stuck a pin in a doll. Mari and Sally followed. I sat there and waited for the results to be revealed.

"I'm sorry to say, Maxim, that you have been expelled from the house." Baron Samedi's expression turned grim as he told the results. As

I stood, Mari walked up to me and stuffed something in my hand.

As the amulet touched my hand, it cooled then warmed. "I can't take this." I held out my hand, revealing the necklace.

She closed my hand around the stone. "Yes, you can. It will protect you out there."

"But you will forget who you are, and me."

"As long as I stay in the house and let the magic keep me safe, I'll remember. Then if I win, I'll remember forever."

She kissed me and then pushed me away.

As I walked toward the door, Saul jumped on my shoulder. "I'll keep her safe. I promise." He handed me one of his rings. "Here. If you need me, call and I'll come."

"Wait the silver will burn me."

"No, it's infused with a special kind of magic to not hurt the wearer."

He jumped off my shoulder and I walked out the door.

Sixteen

When I stepped outside, the air chilled me. "I'm very sorry to have to tell you this, Maxim, but the house has decided your fate."

"Which is?" I asked.

"Death." His laugh sent chills down my spine.

"Why?" But before I could utter another word a tall man dressed all in black from head to toe stepped forward. He held a double-edged ax.

I glanced back and forth between the two. "This can't be happening."

Baron smiled evilly. "Oh it is. You shouldn't protest."

Before I could protest, the executioner raised his ax and swung. The blade nicked the back of my neck. A cool blanket of protection spread around me. The man in black stood there, slack-jawed. He tried again, but this time his blade didn't even touch the skin.

"What is going on?" Baron inquired.

"Something is blocking my blade," the grim reaper spoke.

As they argued, I took my chance and ran.

"Catch him, don't let him get away," the skeleton man yelled.

I ran and ran, getting farther from them. The sky began to darken. When I stopped running, I wiped the sweat from my brow. Slumping against an oak tree, I tried to steady my breathing. Once I caught my breath, I slid to the base of the tree, my ass landing in the cold wet mud.

"Damn," I wondered aloud. "What about Mari? If she gets kicked out of the house, not only will she forget who she is, but she will be put to death." I sighed and stood. "I need to find my way back to her." When I looked around I saw nothing familiar. I gazed around, seeing nothing but a vast landscape of swamps and cypress trees. The branches swung in the nighttime breeze.

As the full moon passed across the sky, shining brightly the course hair erupted all over my body. "No!" I screamed. I dropped to the ground and let sleep overtake me.

The next morning I rolled over, covered in mud, grass, and leaves. I stretched and sat. The only person who could get me back to the house was Zora. Where in the hell was she? A horrible thought popped into my head. What if Griff had found out about her and did something to her? I had to search for her so we could both get back to the house.

I stood, wiped my jeans off, tied my hair back into a man bun, and set out to find Zora. I still had to be on the lookout for the executioner as well. I didn't think they would let me go that easily. For hours I walked and walked, searching under every rock and inside every small cavern, but nothing.

Soon I came across a cemetery. I sniffed and got the scent of something hurt. Once more I tried to get the scent, but death wrapped its ugly head around me, causing me to lose what I searched for.

"Damn it," I cursed.

As I searched, some more, I saw a hazy figure before me. In a trance, I walked toward it. When I got closer, I noticed it was a woman who looked familiar somehow. Her outfit put her life at the time of the Civil War.

"Hello, my name is Charlotte. I'm the protector of this place. May I help you with something?" She looked a little dazed.

I nodded. "I'm searching for my cat."

"A cat, you say?"

"Yes. She is a magical cat, and was sent on an important mission."

She laughed. "All cats are magical."

"Have you seen her?" I asked again.

She nodded. "I've seen 'a' cat, though not sure if it yours. Most cats don't belong to anyone." She turned away and started to walk off. "I must search for my daughter; she is lost like your cat."

"Your daughter?" I asked.

She nodded and walked away from me. "Follow me, your cat's in here."

I ran through the tall thicket, catching my pants leg on a stray thorn. "Ow," I hollered.

I stopped to check on my leg. The thorn had torn my pants, and blood seeped through the material. I dismissed it, knowing I would heal rather quickly. I shrugged. "I don't have time for this," I muttered and glanced up. The ghost had disappeared. "Charlotte!" I hollered. "Where did you go?"

Nothing but the eerie sound of silence replied. I used my fine-tuned senses to try and find her, or anyone. I looked around for the mausoleum where Charlotte said Zora was, but it had disappeared. "Well, shit!" I exclaimed.

I walked through the thickets, searching, and realized I'd gone in circles.

Up ahead I saw the ghostly figure again. I walked toward her and smiled. "Hello, Charlotte."

She looked stunned. "You know me?"

"We met a couple minutes, or...," I pondered the time, "a couple of hours ago."

She cocked her head, trying to remember me. Then she smiled. "You were looking for a...." She paused. "A cat."

I nodded. "Yes, I was. Do you know where she is?"

I followed her, but my foot landed in a hole and I landed on the ground again. When I looked up, she had disappeared again.

Instead of leaving, I stayed put. As long as I sat there against a tree, the ghost did not reappear. I began to lose hope I'd see her or Zora again.

I stood and started to walk. As I headed north, I saw her again. "Charlotte, is that you?"

She looked at me, and then her face showed recognition. "I know you, yet you have not told me your name."

"My apologies. My name is Maxim Rafferty."

"Nice to meet you, Maxim. Now you were looking for your cat, weren't you?"

"Yes."

She walked ahead of me and a mausoleum appeared in the distance. Fog rolled in and covered it. "Maybe you could help me find my daughter."

"Your daughter?" I asked.

"Her name is Eloise." Sadness crept through her voice.

"You're Eloise's mother?" I exclaimed.

She turned back to me and smiled. "You've seen her?"

"Yes." I thought to myself quickly, *She has no idea she's dead.* And the loa of the dead had lied and didn't bring her to the underworld like Eloise thought.

"Where is she?"

"She's safe."

A glistening tear slid down her face. "Are you sure?"

I nodded.

"Very well, your cat is over here." She waved her hands and a dilapidated old marble mausoleum appeared before us. I followed her inside. Cobwebs hung from every corner. A rat scampered across the uneven cement floor and disappeared in a crack in the floor. The ghost shuddered as she watched it hide.

Over in the corner, huddled in a ball, lay Zora. I ran over to her, sliding on the cement, not worried about the scratches and abrasions I surely got. "Zora, are you okay?"

"She's dead," Charlotte said.

"Dead?" My shocked tone was quickly replaced by anger. "How did this happen? Who did this?"

She shook her head. "I don't know. But I can bring her back."

"You can?" I asked, not believing such a thing.

"Yes, when I was alive—"

"Wait. You remember who you are?" I interrupted her.

She smiled. "Yes, it's how I live, forgetting then remembering. Each day is the same."

"So how can you bring her back?"

"When I was alive I was a powerful witch. Unlike my husband, who pulled from the elements, with my power I can breathe life back into things." She smiled kindly at me.

"How come you waited to bring her back?"

"Because I wanted to make sure she had someone who cared for her." Her lips tugged at the corners, causing her eyes to crinkle. "Since you still searched for her, you care for her."

"I do."

"Well, as you know, cats are known for having nine lives." She indicated Zora. "Though I fear this one has lived over and over many times."

"How many times do you think?"

"Maybe seven or eight, not sure."

My anticipation wavered. "How long will this take?"

"Not very long. Once I give her the initial boost, she'll do the rest." She raised her hands and the candles that probably hadn't been lit for centuries came to life, flickering little flames to and fro. "Good. Now we can begin."

She knelt beside the cat and held her hands over her, chanting a spell....

In this place and in this hour
I call upon a higher power
Return the spirit that too quickly flew

Enter back in the flesh to breathe anew
Without hesitation or concern
That which rose needs to return

Then when she finished she put her mouth over Zora's. An opaque haze sifted from her mouth to the cat's. Charlotte pulled back and sat on her knees. She waited, as did I, though I wasn't nearly as patient as she. The cat stirred a bit, and after about fifteen minutes Zora stretched, then rolled over. Her eyes blinked open.

"Nice to see you," Charlotte spoke to the cat.

"Who are you?"

"Zora, this is Eloise's mother," I replied. The cat's head slowly whipped around. When she saw me, her mouth made an odd shape for a cat. She tried to sit, but I stopped her. "Rest, Zora."

She licked her paw as she lay on her belly. "What are you doing here?"

"Griff made good on his promise to kick me out."

"What happened in the immunity challenge?"

"I won, but he informed me that if I didn't give it to him, he'd kill Mari. In fact, that was his plan the whole time."

"What was?" she purred.

"To turn all the fairies human."

"Oh my, that will be devastation to the world without fairy magic." Her eyes widened as she saw the amulet hanging around my neck. She reached her paw out and swatted it. "She gave you that?"

I nodded. "Thank goodness she did, or I'd be dead."

She cocked her head. "What do you mean?"

I shook my head and scoffed. "Baron tricked us. Once we are kicked out, we are put to death." I sat beside her, letting loose the guilt I'd pushed away about Corbin leaving the house.

Zora sat, leaning her head on my knee. She leaned forward and swatted at the amulet around my neck. "She gave it to you?"

"Yes, and damn it if it didn't save me from Baron's executioner."

She stretched out across the ground beside me. "I'll get you back to her."

I absentmindedly stroked her. "What happened to you?"

"My suspicions are that Griff found out about your plan to save Mari and tried to stop me."

"How did you end up with Charlotte?"

She shook her head. "No idea."

Charlotte interrupted us. "I found you tossed against the mausoleum, left to die."

"So you were never able to get to Mari's realm."

"No. I wasn't."

"Damn." I dropped my head in my hands. "We'll need to get what we can from them. She may not last if we don't."

"Fine, but let me rest before we leave."

Seventeen

Patiently I waited for Zora to wake. As I did, thoughts of Mari plagued me. Was she okay? My heart beat rapidly and my palms sweated at the possibility of what she'd endured in the house since I had left. I hoped Saul was okay as well.

Zora nudged me slightly. "Are you ready?" she purred.

"Yes. Will it take long?" I asked.

"Not if we hurry. I can jump between time and get to different realms if needed."

"Different realms?" I asked.

She nodded, smoothing her whiskers. "I know Cassandra is powerful, but I have a feeling we'll need to see the king. The fairies, I fear, are the only ones that will have what Mari needs."

"Good, because I don't know how much time Mari has in the house."

"Don't worry, he'll take her to the end. He needs her."

"True."

I followed her out of the mausoleum, where Charlotte was waiting for us.

"Maxim...." She paused. "Before I forget who you are....please tell Eloise that I love her."

I nodded. "I will. I promise."

"Charlotte, thanks for saving me." Zora placed her paws in the air, then touched the ghost.

"It was my pleasure to be able to help one as magical as you. I hope you have many more lives to live."

The cat cocked her head. "We'll see," she grinned. "Let's go, Max."

We walked away, and sadness crept all around me as the ghost and the mausoleum disappeared. I shook my head at the thought that when she reappeared she wouldn't remember a thing.

Another thing weighed on my mind. Was Mari okay? I wouldn't be able to live with myself if something bad happened to her.

As I followed Zora, I gazed at my surroundings. Small flashes of life before I escaped sudden death came and went as we walked. What had I gotten myself into? And all because I'd defied my fate, which was to be alpha of my pack.

"Wait, Zora." I stopped and closed my eyes, remembering the first time I'd seen Mari. There she stood as we waited to enter the dark and dank catacombs leading to my freedom. When my turn to enter came, my palms sweated as I followed the fairy through, but she was way ahead of me. She was a petite flower of a creature, someone I couldn't see myself with, but someone that I was drawn to. Her long blonde shimmering hair made me want to run my fingers through it.

I imagined staring into her round blue eyes for days. As I reminisced, something scratched my leg. "Ow!" I opened my eyes and looked around.

"Can you hurry? We should get going."

Zora swatted at me then turned and walked ahead of me. Up ahead I saw something I'd never seen before; it looked like a shimmering tunnel. I quickly followed Zora through it. Before my eyes different realms passed by in the blink of an eye, much like a revolving door. The spinning stopped and we landed amidst huge cypress trees and in the distance, I saw a wooden planked bridge.

"Come, Max."

I followed her toward the bridge and walked along it. At the end stood a small house. Zora's paws barely made a sound as she padded closer.

She stood on her back legs and pawed at the door.

The door opened and a beautiful ebony skinned woman met us. "Hello, Zora." The woman knelt and scratched Zora behind her ears. She purred loudly and leaned into the woman. "Why have you come to visit me? Not that I mind, but something must be wrong."

The cat sat back on its haunches. "Yes, I'm afraid so." She turned to me. "This is Maxim Rafferty. He's a—"

Cassandra interrupted her. "A werewolf. Only not from this part of Louisiana."

"No ma'am, my pack comes from the North Shore. My pack's history stems from a chief of the Lacomb tribe and a Spanish slave woman." I paused as I looked at Cassandra. "But you probably knew that already."

"Ah, I'd heard y'all were still around, though you aren't quite as popular as the Rougaroux that inhabit this area. You must be Eustache Rafferty's son."

I nodded. "You know my father?"

"I know all paranormal creatures. Well, come on in and fill me in on what's happening."

The cat sashayed inside and immediately jumped onto the table. I walked inside and Cassandra shut the door behind us.

Zora sat on the table licking her front paw.

"Please have a seat." Cassandra inclined her hand to the table, but I waited. I'd been taught to only sit after the females had done so. The practitioner smiled and sat. I pulled the chair out and straddled it. The amulet around my neck fell from its hiding spot under my shirt.

"Maxim, where did you get that?"

"From Mariwen. She gave it to me when…." I stopped. "Look, Mari is in trouble, as are all of the fairies."

She gasped. "I should have gone with my gut, and told the king what happened with her family, even though the royal court was dealing with their own tragedy at the time. He deserved to know what was happening in his kingdom." She sighed. "Even though they had informed me of their concern about Duran being banished for disobeying an order. Maybe I could have helped. I do have some sway with the court." She smiled nervously.

"I don't want her to get into trouble," I begged.

She leaned forward, ignoring my plea. "So, you were in the house with Mari."

I nodded. "I was kicked out and escaped sudden death, thanks to this amulet." I clenched it in my hand.

She leaned back in the chair. "Something is weighing on me, though. You come from a long line of werewolves. If you had won, you would have become a regular human. Why would you want that? Being an alpha is a great honor."

I hung my head. "Until now, I never wanted it. But meeting Mari has brought out the power of alpha in me. I'm drawn to protect her."

She touched my chin and brought my head up, looking into my eyes. The corners of her eyes crinkled and her lips curved into a smile. "I think it's more than protecting her. You've fallen in love with her, haven't you?"

"I'm afraid I have. And I know it's forbidden to have these feelings."

"Yes, a forbidden love it is. For now, we'll put that problem on the back burner. What has happened to Mariwen?"

"Griff has poisoned her, causing her to not be able to heal herself. In the house, he's done everything to win, even cheat. He plans on taking the human elixir and increasing it to turn every fairy human."

She stood, knocking her chair to the ground. The clattering sound echoed around the tiny house. A man came running out of the back. "Are you okay, dear?"

She turned and faced him. "I'm fine, Will. Just a bit of terrible news for the fairies."

"Oh no, again? Shall I alert the sentries?"

"No, I think we should wait. They have enough on their plates right now with the princess returning home."

"Very well, dear. But if you change your mind I have your back." He shook his head and returned to the back of the shop.

"So, Will came back from his travels?" Zora asked.

"Yes, he's been back for a couple of weeks. He's been close to the fairies for a long time. You know he senses certain thing especially pain. After the princess left, he dropped what he was researching and returned. It took him a while to return home, but he's back now. Well enough of him...we need to figure out what to do about Mariwen."

"I think it's time to let the king know what is happening in his kingdom," Zora said matter-of-factly.

Cassandra shook her head. "I can't."

"I know you are nervous, but he won't dare be mad at you for keeping such a secret. He needs you and your protection of the fairies."

"Yes, but I didn't protect Mari, did I? I sent her off with evil to destroy all fairies."

"Besides, I fear that the fairies are the only ones who have something to help Mari get back on the mend," Zora said.

I patted her shoulder. "Cassandra, I barely remember stories told about the feu follet when I was younger. From all I've heard of them, they are fair and understanding."

"You are right," she replied. "Will, let's go, we are going to speak to the king."

He came running out of the back with a backpack over his shoulder. "Good. I'm glad you changed your mind." The dark-skinned man stared at us, waiting for us to move. He rubbed his head anxiously.

"You can thank Maxim and Zora."

A smile crept along his face as he saw Zora. "It's been a long time, hasn't it?"

The cat jumped off the table and rubbed against the man's leg. He faced me. "So you're Maxim Rafferty?"

I cocked my head. "You know of me?"

He chuckled. "I, like my wife, know all the paranormal creatures. If you would've stayed and become alpha you would've learned about us." He leaned forward. "Don't worry about your forbidden love of Mari. It will be a long road filled with roadblocks, but—"

Cassandra interrupted him, giving him a side eye. "Let's get going. The sooner we get there, the sooner we can get back to Mari."

The four of us walked out of the shop. When I stepped outside, I lifted my head toward the sky, checking out the moon. As we walked, the darkness cast the shadows into hiding. In the silence, our footsteps echoed on the wooden walkway. Ripples in the water underneath us spread far and wide. Ahead of us at the levee sat a boat, rocking back and forth with the movement of the murky water.

"Let's hurry," Cassandra commanded.

Eighteen

We got into the small boat, and it moved magically through the murky waters of the swamp.

"Will it take long to get there?" I asked.

"Not too long. There is another veil that we can cross through, closer to our location," Cassandra replied.

We rode in silence through the swamp, possibly all our thoughts on the same thing...to save the fairies.

"We are almost there," Will spoke staring out into the distance from the bow.

I leaned forward and saw nothing but trees. "How do you know?"

He smiled. "I can see the veil from here."

I focused but still saw nothing. As the boat moved closer to the levy my heart began to beat faster. Before it docked, I jumped out and splashed through the water. The others joined me on the levee.

"Where to now?" I asked.

Cassandra pointed ahead. "Right through those two trees, the ones with the branches hanging low."

We walked quickly toward them. Zora walked through the veil and the others followed. Suddenly I became apprehensive to cross.

"Come on, Maxim," Zora prodded me.

When I stepped over a burning sensation came from my chest. I grabbed the amulet and it sizzled. "What the hell?"

Cassandra murmured under her breath. As soon as she finished the stone cooled in my hand.

"What did you say?"

"Oh, a little spell. I'm sorry, Maxim. I forgot to have you remove it before entering."

"Why did it do that?"

"Because you are not the fairy it was created for."

"But it protected me when I left the house," I replied.

"That's because this is the fairy realm, which has its own magic."

Zora sat on her haunches, licking her paw. "Look, we need to hurry and let our arrival be known. I'm surprised the sentries aren't here yet. The king has put extra protection out ever since the princess stepped over the veil, and the unfortunate kidnapping of the—"

Cassandra interrupted her and shushed us. As I glanced around I wondered how Mari was able to escape, but a voice interrupted my thoughts.

"Too late."

I spun around. "Who are you?" I asked.

"We are the royal sentries. We are here to protect this realm." At least a dozen sentries had appeared, arms raised, with bows and arrows pointed at only me.

"Eloi, please put that arrow down," Zora demanded.

The sentry looked abashed. "Zora, is that you?"

She padded over to him and rubbed against his leg. "Yes."

"What are you doing with a werewolf?"

"I've been sworn to protect him."

"Yes, but why is 'he' here?" he replied.

"He has news of one of the fairies."

He glared at me. "What could you possibly know about one of our fairies?"

Will stepped closer to the sentry. "Please Eloi, take us to the king. It's imperative that we speak to him as soon as possible."

"Fine, come with us."

I started to walk, but Eloi stopped me. "I have my eye on you." He nudged me with his bow.

Eloi and another flanked me the entire way to the king. I hoped he would be more lenient with me.

We walked through a thickness of oak trees. When we stepped out of them before us was a small pond. Off in the distance, I saw nothing. To the right of me, I saw a shimmering doorway.

"What's that?" I asked, pointing.

"You can see that?" Cassandra asked.

"Yes, why?"

"Because that is another doorway to the human world." She gazed at me and cocked her head. "There seems to be more to you than I first realized. Perhaps you have a touch of magic in you. Though I'm not sure why you couldn't see the other one."

Will whispered, "I sense you are opening your eyes more to magic and its possibilities, even if you don't realize it."

"Maybe." But my mind was on something else. "How are we going to get across this water?"

Will smiled. "By fairy, of course."

"No way...they aren't strong enough to carry us."

"Pfttt says you," Eloi scoffed.

Before I could protest, Eloi grabbed me by the shoulders and flew off with me. The others followed behind us. Eloi kept ahold of me, but when the water disappeared and lush green land appeared he dropped me with a thud. I glared at him, but he turned his back on me. I stood and dusted myself off.

Zora and the others were set gently on the ground. A crowd of fairies gathered around us, murmuring. I glanced around and everyone stared at me.

A tall man with white hair emerged from the crowd as it parted. The sentries stood on either side of him, except Eloi, who kept close to me.

"Cassandra, why have you brought a werewolf to my realm? We've had enough strangers coming through the veil." A hint of anger mixed with curiosity laced his question.

"I'm very sorry, but he has news about one of your fairies."

From my peripheral vision, I saw three fairies huddled together, fear crossing their faces, and their body language showed a sense of nervousness.

The king stepped forward. "What is your name?"

"Maxim Rafferty."

He crossed his arms over his chest. "Ahh, you are from the Lacomb pack?"

"Yes. You know of my pack?"

He nodded. "I know of them and your father, but only from their reputation. Your father has always been revered as a kind alpha. Nothing like what we must deal here with the Rougaroux. Who, I may add, have come into my realm and caused disarray. Come with me and tell me what information you have."

We followed him as the crowd dispersed around us. Ahead I saw a lavish castle, complete with marble steps leading to huge wooden cypress doors.

"How do others not know this place exists?" I asked the king as I glanced around at my surroundings.

He chuckled. "Because humans don't really believe in magic anymore. Well, all but one...my daughter is married to a human."

I gasped but quickly laughed. "Really? And you allowed that?"

"You haven't met my daughter; she is strong-willed. She has never been one to follow the rules."

With his confession to me, I suddenly had hopes he would not dismiss my feelings for Mari.

I nodded and followed him. We walked through different hallways until we stopped at a door. Inside sat a beautiful brunette female. She never even looked in our direction, as her head was buried deep in a book.

"Alicia, would you please excuse us?"

She glanced up and smiled. "Sure thing, Father. I should go visit Cole anyway." She stood and walked past me, but stopped. "Who's this?"

"Maxim Rafferty."

"Why's he here?" Her question wasn't rude but more curious. "I thought since the kidnapping you weren't allowing any more strangers past the veil."

"He has some news about one of the fairies." He paused. "You wouldn't know anything about this, would you?" he asked sternly.

Nineteen

She blushed as if she may know something. "Well...," she stuttered. "I've heard rumblings since I've come back."

King Roi cocked his head. "What sort of, uh, rumblings?" he asked.

"Just that...." Her face turned a bright shade of red. "Well, when I left—"

Before she could utter another word the door slammed open. One of the fairies I'd seen earlier came rushing in. "I'm sorry, King...." She stopped, and her eyes brimmed with tears streaming down her face. She pulled a white handkerchief from her pocket and wiped them away.

He walked over to her. "No worries, Erline, but as your king please tell me what has you in such a tizzy."

"First, can I ask the werewolf a question?" She inclined her head to me. The king nodded and she walked over to me. "Is she all right?"

I feared to tell her the truth, so I lied. "She's fine for now, but I need to return to her soon." My anxiety showed through my tone.

"Why?" She smiled at me.

"Because I care about her."

She patted me on the forearm. "Good."

"Ahem." The king cleared his throat and we both turned our heads in his direction. He smiled and waved us over to have a seat. After we were sitting on the sofa, he asked, "Now what's going on?"

Before Erline could answer a young man no older then my little sister stepped forward. I whispered to Zora, "Is that Mari's brother?"

"Yes. And I fear what the king will do if he tells the truth," the cat purred.

The young man knelt on one knee and bowed his head and placed a fist over his heart. "I'm sorry, my—"

"Don't Duran, please." Erline began to sob.

The king smiled kindly but authoritatively. "Tell me what's going on here in my kingdom."

Duran looked in my direction, as if trying to figure out how much of his problems I was privy to then continued. "When the princess left, even though we sentries were told not to leave, I did."

"You what?" the king boomed loudly.

Mari's brother jumped from the sound. "I'm sorry, my king, but I didn't want her to be hurt. My job is protecting the members of this kingdom."

"Well, you know for your blatant disregard to a direct order you will have to—"

Father," the princess spoke. "He was trying to find me." She walked over and slipped an arm through his. "Don't be too hard on him."

The king, who still stood, changed his angry expression at the behest of his daughter. "Fine, but I shall talk to Eloi about some sort of punishment." He squeezed his daughter's hand. "How's that?"

"You're the best." She beamed at him.

"Anyway, I should be ashamed of things. I'm the one who's sorry. If I had warned any of y'all about the consequences of leaving, maybe none of my kingdom would have been hurt. But I, like you, had everyone's best interests at heart."

I leaned forward, interrupting. "I know this is all very interesting, and I don't mean to be disrespectful, but we have bigger problems. May I speak to you alone, please?"

The king turned to me, then spoke to the others. "I'll keep you abreast of the situation here. Duran, please take your mother and father home."

He stood and bowed. "Yes, sire."

"No. If this is about my daughter I need to know," Erline spoke defiantly.

I glanced at the king, who just stared back at me. "It's your decision."

I sighed deeply. "All right...I lied, Mariwen is in trouble. But for me to tell you what happened," I grabbed a hold of Erline's hand, "you must be willing to tell why she's out of the realm."

She covered her mouth and gasped lightly. "You know?"

"Yes, I had to find out so I could protect her."

"But you aren't protecting her, you're here," Duran shouted.

"Quiet, son," the fairy chastised him. "If your sister hadn't been trying to protect you she wouldn't be in this situation."

"So, the fairy you have come to tell me about must be Erline's daughter." The king cocked a brow at me

I nodded. "Yes, Mariwen is in trouble."

Erline came forward as her husband stared at me stoically. "Wait I thought you said she was safe." Her disappointment in my lie sucker punched me in the gut.

"I'm sorry I lied."

Her expression softened. "I assume you did so to protect us."

I nodded. "Yes."

She sat beside me and held my hand. "King Roi, when Duran left, since he didn't have his memory we were worried about him so much that we betrayed you." She never wavered as the king frowned at her.

"How?" he asked.

"We didn't know any other way but to ask a bounty hunter dragon for help." Still, she sat there, never flinching as the anger grew evident on his face.

"Which one?" the king asked.

"Griff...."

"You went to Griff Warwick of the dragon bounty hunters?" the king asked in shock.

"You know of him?"

"Yes, his family and mine go back centuries. He used to protect us, but now he's bent on destroying us," he said, pacing back and forth.

Erline started to sob uncontrollably. "We're so sorry. You had just gotten your daughter back, and we didn't want to add fuel to the fire by telling you what had happened."

"I wish you had come to me. Am I that much of a tyrant?" His voice saddened.

Erline stood and knelt beside the king. "No, you aren't, but we didn't want our family to disappoint you. That is the one thing we could never come back from." She sighed. "But we have done this anyway with our actions."

"It's not their fault." Mari's father spoke for the first time ever. "We were terrified to let the kingdom know what Duran had done by disobeying a direct order. His life is to be a sentry. It's all he's ever wanted. We didn't want to cause you any more stress. Now we've lost our daughter as a result."

"What do you mean?" the king inquired. "This can't be good if Griff is involved."

I patted Erline's hand. She took a deep breath and sat back beside me. "After he retrieved Duran, he informed us of his payment."

"Which was?"

"He wanted Mari."

"He what? He wants a fairy? For what?" All the questions rambled out of his mouth as he sat there in shock.

A wave of sadness overwhelmed me. Erline dropped her focus to her lap and I spoke. "I'm afraid I have more bad news. Before I tell you though, no one could have known his plans, not even her family. I met Mariwen in a place called the Mystical Mansion."

They all looked at me in confusion.

"What's that?" Erline asked.

"It's a house where paranormal creatures battle to win their mortality."

"Why would anyone not want to be what they are?" the princess asked in shock with a quizzical expression.

"I did because I was running away from becoming alpha of my pack." Despair laced my tone, and I now regretted my actions.

"So is Mari still there?" her mother asked.

"Yes...." I paused and squeezed her hand. Zora jumped on my lap

"You need to tell him."

"I can't," I blurted out, causing the rest of the people to gawk at me.

"Can't what?" the king asked.

I sighed and reluctantly continued. "Griff didn't take Mariwen to wed her. He wants her as leverage. He plans on using her against you. He wants to make a mortality elixir." I paused, hating to say the rest. "To make all fairies human."

The king dropped his head, but slowly raised it to stare at Erline and her family. "You have brought dishonor to the kingdom with your selfish actions. You brought my enemy into my kingdom." He stood, knocking over his chair, and yelled, "Get out!"

"We didn't know," she said through tears. Once again she dabbed at her face.

"Let's go." Erline's husband grabbed her hand.

She stood, but before they could leave a beautiful woman resembling the princess entered. "Please stay, we will fix this." She turned to the king. "Dear, don't be angry with them. If you had told the kingdom what happened so long ago this wouldn't have happened." She walked over to me. "I don't think we've been formally introduced. I'm Queen Zenobia."

I stood and took her offered hand and kissed it softly. "Nice to meet you, I'm Maxim—"

She smiled, interrupting me. "I know who you are." She then faced the king. "Roi, you can't take out your frustrations on them. Like you, they were trying to protect their family."

"But they should have come to—" She shook her head, causing him to stop mid-word. He relented and righted his chair, and sat. "Yes, I suppose."

She smiled and stood beside him. "Now Maxim, how can we help Mariwen?"

I shook my head. "I'm not sure. She's been poisoned with iron."

Gasps resonated around the room. "How long has she been sick?"

"Long enough." I sighed. "Even one of our fellow housemates, an elf, was able to pull some of the toxins out of her, but she continued to get worse."

"The reason she's not healing is that something is stopping the good magic inside her," Erline said.

"But I healed outside of the realm," the princess interjected.

Erline turned to the princess. "Yes dear, but yours wasn't a magical ailment."

"So what can we do?" the princess asked.

Erline stood and pressed her dress down. "The only scenario is to meet with the old ones. She needs some fresh fairy magic, especially after being outside of the realm for so long." She wiped away a tear. "I would like to see them...that is, with the king's permission, of course." She smiled nervously and waited patiently for his response.

The king still looked angry, but also seemed complacent. "Fine, go."

The queen patted him on the shoulder and smiled kindly at them.

I stood. "I would like to accompany them if it's at all possible."

Erline spoke up. "It would be helpful if he was able to learn how to give her the cure."

The king nodded. "Other creatures are not permitted inside the sanctuary of the elders, but since you are the son of Eustache's son, I'll allow it." He stopped, contemplating his next words. "Only on one condition."

"Which is?"

"That you never breathe a word of what you see inside the sanctuary, and that you bring Mariwen back to the realm and forget about her afterward."

I choked back a gasp. "What? Why are you punishing us?"

"Don't look at it as a punishment, but more of me protecting my kingdom."

"I don't understand. Why would I? I love her."

"Because it's for her protection. You will one day be the alpha of your pack. There will be no room for a fairy from my realm in your world."

"But Father, you've allowed me to marry a human," the princess interjected.

"Yes, but Maxim's responsibilities to his pack outweigh your predicament. Besides, you've made some sacrifices for your love for Cole, haven't you?"

"Yes, Father."

"Good. Now, there will be no more defiance from anyone." He turned to me. "What do you say?"

Deep down I didn't want to agree, but I had to for Mari. "Yes, all right. I agree."

Zora nudged me and I looked at her. "It might be for the best, Max." Though as she licked her paws I sensed she didn't believe what she said.

I sighed and followed Erline out of the room.

Twenty

We walked in silence down a long corridor. At the end a door lead outside.

"Hurry, Maxim," Erline prodded me.

"How much longer?" I asked as we moved along a narrow gravel walkway. The sky above us dimmed as the sun slid slowly behind the trees. As darkness grew the pathway lit up by way of a dozen or so tiny balls of light, bouncing to and fro. As I peered inside the orbs, small faces looked out at me.

"You have lightning bugs illuminating the path?"

She turned to me and chuckled. "Is that what you call them? We call them fairies; in fact, they are babies."

"Wait, but they are so young. What about their parents?"

"They are not as young as they look. Their parents check on them regularly." She leaned down and let one fly to her finger, and that was when I could see the tiny ball with a tiny fairy inside. It flapped its wings furiously. "They are being trained to become sentries."

"But they are so young."

She smiled kindly. "Becoming a sentry is important, and they must be trained from birth. If you look up into the trees," she pointed in a direction of lights, "you can see some hidden as well."

I squinted my eyes and saw bigger ones. "Are they older?"

"Yes, they start out along the pathway and graduate into the trees. Finally, if they have passed all the tests, they will become protectors of the realm."

One flew and landed on my shoulder. A tiny tinkling of glass bounced off the ball of light. When I looked over at it, I saw a young girl inside, her multicolored wings flapping furiously. She looked angry. Her mouth opened and shut, but I couldn't make out a single word.

"Sienna, he's okay. The king has allowed him here."

"What is she saying?" I asked.

The fairy in the orb stomped her foot and floated off.

"Sentries can be girls?"

She stopped and laughed. "Yes." She looked around. "Thanks to the princess. She opened the king's eyes to certain things."

I thought to myself, *Maybe I can appeal to the king about Mari through the princess. For now, I will do what I can to get her what she needs.*

In the distance I saw a small cottage near the edge of the bayou. "Is that the sanctuary?"

"Yes." She continued to walk along the path, the fairy ahead of us stopped moving... On closer inspection, I saw her arms crossed.

"Sienna, you may keep watch, but he will not hurt the elders."

Sienna eyed me and followed us closely. Erline stopped to pick some flowers.

"Sorry about Sienna, but she has to work harder to be a sentry, being a girl and all. Some of the older sentries do not want a girl as a sentry."

"I can understand that to a point. It's a male position to be the protector."

She laughed. "Don't let Princess Alicia hear you say that."

The fairy flew in front of me. She stopped and pointed her finger at me and mouthed something I couldn't make out. "I'm sorry, Sienna, I meant no disrespect."

She shook her head and turned her back on me tapping her foot.

"Come on, Maxim. She'll get over it."

We followed the walkway to the house and Erline knocked on the door. The door creaked open, and I followed the matronly fairy inside. The quiet house gave off an eerie sensation.

"Where are the elders?" I whispered.

"Shh. In the next room, I assume." She kept walking, her dress not making a single sound as it brushed against the hardwood floors. In the next room, a bunch of old fairies were sitting around a card table.

"You cheated, Minerva."

"No, I didn't."

"Yes, you did."

The fairy stood, caught us in her sight, and tossed the cards on the table. "You need to not be such a sore loser at Bourre, Isadore. Now, ladies, we have company."

They all stood, causing the table to topple over. "We are sorry, where are our manners? Hello, Erline." One of the fairies came over to us.

"Oh, who do we have here?" The others eyed me.

"I'm Maxim—"

"Psh, we know who you are."

"How does everyone know who I am?"

"Maxim, they are the elders...they know all."

"Yes, we do, even of your children's actions, Erline." The fairy dropped her head. "Don't be ashamed."

"Thank you, Minerva."

"Now for the reason, the wolf is here. Come sit, Maxim." I followed them over to the sofa. "How sick is Mariwen?"

"You know she is sick?"

"We weren't sure until you showed up here. Isadore has visions, but they are sometimes hazy."

"Minerva, we need a tea made from lily flower petals."

"Ahh, the healing powers of our sacred flower. Though, we'll need more to help Mariwen. Augustine and Flossie, please grab some cattails and Spanish moss and meet us in the kitchen."

They left the room and Isadore turned to me. "Come with us. Oh, and we know of your terms from the king for coming here. Would you like us to help you with forgetting Mariwen?" She leaned into me. "I sense it'll be hard for you, wolf."

I thought long and hard. "I couldn't bear to totally have her erased from my memory."

"If you change your mind let me know."

I nodded my head and entered a huge kitchen that didn't look like it should fit in the house, yet it did. A marble island sat in the middle of the room, a dozen or so glass bottles and fur-lined bags placed neatly on the surface. The two fairies joined us.

"Now, before we start you have only a little time to get this to her before it'll no longer help her. Can you do this?"

"Sure we can," Zora squealed as she jumped on the counter.

"When did you get here?"

"A few moments ago."

"Zora, how are you?" Flossie patted her on the head.

"I'm good. Sorry, it's been awhile since I've visited."

"You're forgiven. Wait right here while I get you a treat."

"Make sure it's fresh," Zora told her as she retreated, then turned to me. "Last time I visited she gave me a freeze-dried lizard." She stuck her tongue out in a disgusted way, and said, "Pulease. I need my prey wiggly and squirming."

"I remember that Flossie had just discovered freeze drying food and thought she'd try it out on Zora."

The cat shook her head. "It was the most disgusting thing I'd ever tasted."

Flossie came back holding a live lizard by the tail as it wiggled back and forth in her fingers. The moment she let go, Zora dashed after it. She skittered off the counter, causing a couple of bottles to crash to the floor. The fairies laughed and turned their attention to the stove, where a cast iron kettle sat perched over a small flame.

"All right, let's get this tea made and Maxim back on his way."

I watched as the fairies gently pulled the petals from the lily stems. They chopped them very fine and put them aside. Next came the cattails. The seeds were plucked from the stalks and placed in a bowl. Then the stalks were put into the kettle on the stove and a little peppermint was added. The scent of mint floated through the house. I watched as Isadore crushed the seeds and petals together in a mortar with the little marble pestle.

"Almost done," Minerva spoke, and she waved her hand over the boiling kettle and inhaled the fumes. I stood and looked at the contents of the flowers. Isadore had made a paste out of the ingredients.

"How is it possible to make a paste out of petals and seeds?" I asked.

She smiled. "Fairy magic is a wondrous thing, wolf," she leaned in and whispered. "Though this magic only works with a secret ingredient."

"Which is?" I asked.

She didn't answer, just smiled at me. The other fairy, who hadn't spoken yet, faced to Erline.

"Have you saved any tears?"

She nodded. "Yes, Augustine." She shakily reached into her pocket and pulled out the handkerchief she had used earlier to wipe her tears away.

The fairy took the white handkerchief, which I noticed had a silvery substance on it. She placed a crystal glass on the counter in front of her and squeezed the material. Before my eyes, tiny opalescent drops fell into the glass, making tinkling noises against the side.

Augustine handed the handkerchief back to Erline and picked up the glass. "I think this is plenty." She shook it gently, causing the tears to break and turn to liquid, which she poured into the marble mortar. Then Isadore mixed everything until it was a smooth paste.

Minerva opened the cabinet beside me and pulled out a metal container. "Now for the tea. In this instance we'll use a nice chamomile tea...it will help relax her and let the toxins leave her body." She smiled at me, then took a small glass orb out of another cabinet and placed it gently on the counter. Raising her hand, a small portion of the orb rose and she filled it with the water concoction. I watched as she then opened a drawer and pulled out a metal contraption with holes. Quickly she poured the tea leaves inside and closed it tightly. Through the little hole, she dropped the tea leaves inside. In an instant, the water changed colors from white to red, then finally white again. The scent of peppermint wafted through the house.

Minerva turned to me. "The tea should be well infused by the time you get to Mariwen."

"What about the—?"

"Oh, that will dissolve."

"Really? It looks like metal."

"Looks can be deceiving." She grinned, then added the paste. Pink and white swirled again as the flower mixture melted into the tea, though the colors never settled. She placed the lid back on and scooped it up in her hands. I wondered if it was hot to the touch. As the thought came

Minerva spoke. "It won't burn you, but it will stay hot. But you only have until daybreak before it loses its magic, so you shouldn't dilly dally." She placed the orb in a fur-lined bag and handed it to me.

I held it close to me.

"Maxim, you don't have to hold it tightly. The bag will protect it. In fact, you can put it in your pocket." Flossie giggled.

I looked at her in shock. "But it will break."

"Just try it."

Hesitantly I tried to shove it in my pocket, and it slid effortlessly inside.

"The wonders of fairy magic." She smiled at me. "Now hurry back to Mariwen and bring her back to us."

The three fairies took turns, each hugging me goodbye. I noticed Isadore pulling a bag out of her pocket. It wiggled, causing the bag to move to and fro.

"Here Zora, for later," she grinned. The feline took it in her mouth and held it tight. The bag kept moving but slowly stopped. I laughed at the thought that the lizard had no chance at all of living.

Before we left Isadore leaned in closer and held me tightly. "Remember what I said. If you change your mind about truly forgetting Mariwen, let me know. Let Zora know and she can get in touch with me. Sometimes it's for the best."

"I'll think about it, but honestly, I don't mind the burden of remembering her."

She smiled at me. "She is one of a kind, isn't she?"

Minerva interrupted us. "You must hurry."

The others waited patiently as we pulled back and headed away from the cottage.

Twenty-One

Erline, Zora, and I hurried along the lighted path. Sienna led the way, no doubt in a hurry to get rid of me. We walked around the castle and two otters chattered from a small pool beside it. As we rounded the corner we were met by Cassandra, Will, and the king.

"I hope you have gotten what you needed."

"Yes, Your Majesty, I did."

"Good. Once you save Mariwen from Griff I'd like her returned here."

I didn't dare tell him getting her out of the house would be a deathly problem. We headed quickly back to our little boat. Through the entire trip back I remained quiet, thinking of how I'd have to forget about Mari. I didn't know if I could do it. Maybe, just maybe, I could come up with a plan. After all, the king had allowed his daughter to marry a human. Zora curled into my lap while

I contemplated a way to get out of the promise I'd given the fairy king.

"We are here." Cassandra's voice pulled me from my thoughts.

I stood and stretched my stiffened legs, but I forgot that Zora had been on my lap. She clawed at me as she slipped to the bottom of the boat.

"I'm sorry, Zora."

"Sure you are," she hissed.

I stepped out of the boat and headed to leave.

"Wait, Maxim, I have something for you." Cassandra's expression softened as she sensed my frustration. "Don't worry, it won't take long. Will, can you give me his present?"

"Sure thing, dear." He pulled a wooden box from his bag over his shoulder and handed it to me.

"What's this?"

"Open it, Maxim." Cassandra smiled at me.

I slid the top off, and inside, perched on a bed of red suede, was a beautiful pocket knife. "A pocket knife?" I questioned.

"Not just a pocket knife," she hinted smugly.

The hilt was a beautiful blue crystal. I traced the suede with my fingertips and picked up the knife. When I clicked on the lock button the blade slid out to reveal an exquisitely intricate design covering the length of the steel. "This is beautiful," I exclaimed. I flipped the blade over and over, blinking and squinting my eyes.

Beautiful curly letters in what looked like Latin flowed across the blade. "Is this...?"

"Yes. You can read Latin, can't you?"

I nodded. "Of course."

"Good. When you read the inscription on the blade it will open to reveal a sword, the only thing that will truly kill your enemy. You must find your enemy's weakness in order for it to work. I also have an amulet I made especially for you." She pulled out a leather cord. From it dangled a blue crystal. "Here, let me put it on you." The moment it touched my skin a calming effect surrounded me. "The crystal is a blue kyanite. Maxim, this stone will help restore your body's balance and harmony. I fear you have a battle ahead of you. Did you sense a calmness when I put it on you?"

I nodded. "Yes, as a matter of fact, I did."

"If you focus all your energy on the crystal it will help you achieve anything you wish." Will leaned in closer. "If you concentrate hard enough you may even be able to cloak yourself. Then and only then you can reveal yourself when needed."

"Thank you," I told them.

Cassandra hugged me tightly. "Be on your way. You have only a few hours of dark left."

The trip back to the house happened in a blur. When my feet touched the ground, I steadied myself and looked around. The graveyard sat before us. The scent of death and decay permeated my nostrils. Up ahead I saw Charlotte.

"How much farther from here?" I asked Zora.

She grinned. "Through the graveyard. Max, this is part of the original house."

"It is?"

"Yes."

I blinked my eyes and saw a hazy scene unfold before me, a beautiful garden with flowers and trees. "Is this the garden where Eloise played?"

"You can see it?"

I nodded. "It's a bit out of focus, but yes."

"I'm sure it is. It looks different to us because we're not part of their deaths."

Charlotte floated toward us. She cocked her head as if she was trying to recognize us.

"Hello, Charlotte."

"You know me?" she asked.

"Yes. I hate to be rude, but I'll let Eloise know you are okay."

"You know my daughter?" Her questions bombarded me, but I started to walk faster. Zora ran ahead of me. When she did, I saw a faint outline of the house before us. "Shit, I was here the whole time."

"Yes, everything here is something of an illusion. It's how Eloise's father wanted it. Some paranormal creatures are more in tuned to the magic."

I touched the amulet that was nestled underneath my shirt. "Maybe or maybe it's a bit of voodoo magic."

"Could be. Now hurry, we must get to the house. We still have a way to go, and the sun will be rising soon."

She darted off and I ran to keep pace with her. The house seemed to get farther away, but after what seemed like an hour, we arrived at a door. I heard the clicking of the cameras moving. "Wait, Zora."

"Why?"

I pointed to the moving camera a short distance away. She glanced up at it, and as soon as she did, the door opened. Vanity stepped out of the house.

"Shit. It must be the day to expel a houseguest." I sucked in a deep breath and clutched the kyanite stone around my neck. With all my concentration, I willed myself to become invisible. But before I could rush toward the elf she blinked out of sight. The executioner looked probably as confused as he had with me. Zora crouched low to the ground a few feet from the door, which I noticed remained open.

"Maxim, hurry before the door closes."

I held my breath as I saw the skeletal man look in my direction and smile. Quickly I ran toward the door and followed Zora inside. "Damn it, do you think he saw me?"

"Probably. There really is no way to hide from Baron. To be honest with you, I think he has a fondness for you."

"I sure to hell hope so, because I'd hate to see what would happen to me if he finds out I'm back."

"We don't have time to worry about that; we need to find Mariwen," Zora chastised me.

As we headed through the hallway, footsteps resounded behind me. "Oh no, Maxi, are you dead?" Eloise squealed.

I turned and faced her. Her mouth turned upside down and she started to pout. "Shhh, Eloise, I'm not dead," I whispered.

"Are you sure?" she poked me.

"Eloise, dear, please don't poke him. You may cause him to lose his focus on remaining invisible," Zora told her as she sat staring at us.

"Ely, can you go get Mari and Saul for me and bring them to the secret room?"

"Are you sure? She's, uh—" Zora interrupted her by shaking her head. She saluted me. "Yes, sir." In a flash, she disappeared.

As I walked through the house, keeping an eye out for Griff, a voice from behind startled me. "What secret room?" Saul asked.

I grinned wide at the sight of my best friend. "Damn, I missed you."

"I missed you too. Man, am I glad you're back." Saul slapped me on the thigh. "I snuck outside after you left and saw the executioner with Baron."

"Yeah, yeah, it was a close call. I'm sure that he's going to be pissed at me if he finds me back here," I said as I chanced a peek around the corner and signaled Saul to follow me. I sensed someone watching us, but I shoved it away. Quickly I opened the panel in the wall and we entered the tunnel. A spooky sensation wrapped around me as we maneuvered toward the room. Up ahead a dim light illuminated the walkway. "Hurry, it's up ahead."

We waited in the secret room for Mari to come. Pacing back and forth became my modus operandi.

"Maxim, Mari's different." Saul sighed and patted me on the thigh.

"What do you mean?" I questioned.

"It's almost as if she's forgotten who or what she is."

"That can't be possible." Panic ensued, and I reached into my pocket and clutched the orb.

"Well, you've been gone for a while."

Shock rolled off me. "By my calculations, I wasn't gone but maybe a week."

He shook his head. "No, time is measured differently in here."

I glanced at the clock and the minutes ticked by. "Where could she be?" My legs gave out and I collapsed into a nearby chair that had magically moved under me. "What if...?"

My question was repeated back to me, but not by the fairy I'd fallen in love with. Instead by someone resembling her, though she stared at me with coldness in her eyes. Dark circles underlined her eyes. She blinked, then returned to the stoic gaze.

"What do you want?" she asked angrily.

Eloise stood beside her, a little scared.

My eyes brimmed with tears and my chest constricted. "I've brought you something to ease your mind and help heal you." I pulled the orb from my pocket, and it enlarged in my hand as I unwrapped the soft material encasing it.

"Did you get that from...?" She stopped, already knowing the answer. Quickly her facial expression softened, but it only lasted seconds. Deep down I sensed something was wrong with her.

"What did Griff do to you?" I asked. Without hesitation, I grasped her small hand in mine. Her skin burned mine. "You're still hot to the touch." I raised my other hand and touched her forehead, but she backed away from my touch. As she tried to pull away, I gripped her tighter. "What's wrong with you?"

She tugged her hand free. "Nothing."

She lied as I gazed deep into her blue eyes. Behind her callus façade blared a heart-wrenching sadness.

"Look, you need to drink this tea. Your mom and the elders made it for you."

"You saw my mom...?" She sniffed back a sob.

I nodded and handed her the tea. "Hurry, before it gets cold."

She took it hesitantly. Her hands shook as she held the orb and popped the lid off. As she put it to her lips, I saw the liquid deplete as she drank. Suddenly, though, it flew from her grasp and crashed to the floor, spilling what was left of the concoction on the floor. It seeped into the concrete floor and disappeared.

I spun around to see Griff staring angrily at us. "How did you find this place?" I asked.

"No, the question is how the hell did you get back inside?" he grimaced.

A smile crossed my face. "Magic."

"Well, then I'll be happy to have you removed from the house again." He opened his mouth and blew a fireball in my direction. I dodged out of the way just in the nick of the time.

"You fucker," I screamed at him as I righted myself.

He stalked over to me and grabbed me by the scruff of my shirt. "Who are you calling a fucker?" He shook me like a rag doll, causing my glasses to slip off my face and land on the floor. I sucker punched him in the nose. His head bounced back, but he held his grip on me.

"Let me go, asshole," I screamed, spittle flying all over. He dragged me out of the room, crushing my eyeglasses as he exited. The glass crunched under his feet. I glanced back at Mari. Her face showed sadness and she mouthed, "I'm sorry."

Saul scrambled after me and kicked Griff in the shin. "Let him go," he hollered.

Griff plucked him away as if he was a gnat. "This is not your fight, garden worm."

My feet shuffled against the floor as he dragged me through the tunnel. "Zora, please get in touch with my dad."

Griff bellowed out a rough laugh. "Your father can't help you now. Besides, he'll never be allowed in the house." He picked me up, dangled me from the ground, and eyed me. "You should have stayed home, or at least not come back here," he spat.

Don't worry, Maxim, I'll make sure he gets into the house somehow, she spoke in my head, and then dashed off. Hopefully, she would return with him soon.

When we exited from the secret tunnel, we were met by Baron. Griff tossed me to the floor, where I landed at the boots of the skeleton man.

He grinned. "Nice to see you back, Maxim." I couldn't tell if he meant that or if he planned on killing me this time.

Twenty-Two

In anger, I glanced at the skeleton man. "Are you going to kill me this time?"

He shook his head, then offered me his hand. I refused it, so he knelt and whispered to me, "Please come with me."

Begrudgingly I took his offered hand. His white gloves were soft to the touch, but still his bones pressed into mine. Once I stood again, he turned to the dragon. "Griff, I've got this now."

He glared at me. "Fine, but if he escapes again I will kill him."

He turned back to face the dragon and narrowed his eyes. "You'd better watch your tone with me. Remember, I can end you like that." He snapped his fingers. Griff slinked back a bit. Apparently, the loa was the only thing that scared him. "That's better. You're not in charge here." He led me off. "Before you ask me, no, I'm not going to kill you."

I stopped suddenly. "Why not?"

"Well, to be honest, I'm rather pissed you got away from my executioner. But, the way I see this playing out now, I will get to enjoy more now than I would have enjoyed killing you. I'd love to see how this goes. Will Griff kill you or will you kill him...?" He paused and grinned. "Or will the fairy be the one to end either one of you?"

He opened the door and the cool air hit me. I sucked in a deep breath as the stench of death and decay surrounded me. "Where are you taking me?"

He grinned at me. "Somewhere you'll be protected until the last master of domain challenge."

I hesitantly followed him deep into the cemetery. Ghosts flitted everywhere. The branches of the trees reached out to me. I ducked from one and fell to the ground. I pushed myself back into a standing position, noticing the branch was wrapped around the trunk of the tree. The moss hung from the upper branches and danced to and fro before my eyes. "What is this place?"

He waved his hands around. "A place I've created to be hidden from the others. You see, Griff is set on taking your life."

"Why do you care?"

He pondered this question for a time. "Because it gives me excitement to screw with people's lives." He laughed as he rounded the corner of a huge mausoleum. For one instant I thought about running. I backed up, but an invisible force stopped me. The skeleton man shook his finger at me. "Tsk tsk, Maxim, please don't anger me." With a wave of his hand, I was pulled closer to him, the toes of my boots dragging against the dirt.

The door to the crypt creaked as it opened. Baron shoved me inside, where a prison cell magically appeared. I slid against the dirt and the steel door closed and locked behind me. Quickly I stood and turned around, my hands gripping the steel bars. "Let me out of here, now." I pulled but they didn't budge.

He bowed, then tipped his hat. "Not yet, but soon." He turned on his heels and left.

"Damn it!" I screamed.

I slumped to the floor and tried to keep my anger at bay. But it didn't work, and in mere seconds the stubble of hair grew along my arms. My canines slid effortlessly out, and I howled. I wondered if my anger was causing this premature shift.

"Settle down, friend."

At the familiar voice, I glanced around and saw Saul standing there with his arms crossed.

"I can't," I huffed and stepped back from the bars.

"Damn, dude, is that what you look like in shifter form?" I glanced down and saw my jeans still intact, knowing my bottom was human and my top half was wolf. He stifled a laugh as he somehow squeezed through the steel bars and walked over to me.

"How did you do that?"

He grinned hugely. "Magic." He handed me my glasses, which were miraculously fixed.

"How...?"I stopped, already knowing the answer.

Saul stared up at me. "Now sit, we need to talk."

"About what?"

"Mari."

"Yes, do you think she got enough of the tea?" I asked as I slumped to the floor and sighed.

"We've got bigger problems. First please take a deep breath, because I don't want you going full shift on me after I fill you in."

I looked at him, remembering the weird way she had acted toward me. She'd seemed angry like she didn't recognize me. "What happened to her?"

He looked at my chest where the amulet sat. He touched it, then shook his head. He squatted beside me. "When you left, Mari was devastated. She ran from the house, but not into the yard where we do competitions. She ran out the front door. Right after she left the house I grabbed her back inside, but the damage had already been done." He dropped his head. "I'm sorry I failed you in protecting her."

I listened, and as he told me, it made my chest ache for her. "So, what happened when you brought her back inside?"

He pointed towards the necklace then touched it "She should have had this on her when she left the house. In those few seconds she stepped into the human world, it changed her life."

"How much of it is gone?"

"She knows her name, but she doesn't remember that she's a fairy. Also, her wings are gone."

"No!" I screamed out. When I regained my composure, I looked over to Saul. "We need to get her back home. It's the only place she can regain what she's lost."

"How do you propose we do that?" He scowled at me.

I shook my head. "No idea. Maybe once my father gets here he can help us. I'm also afraid that without the tea from her realm she will keep getting sicker and eventually die."

We sat in silence, contemplating our next moves in this so-called game. I pulled my hair back into a man bun and shoved my glasses further back on my nose.

Zora sashayed into the room. "Did you get word back to my dad?"

She nodded, and behind her stood my dad.

Twenty-Three

"Hello, son." He sounded grim as he walked inside the mausoleum.

I glanced up and an insurmountable disappointment from him befell me. Zora zig zagged between his legs, stopping suddenly to rake her nails down his pants leg. He grimaced while waiting patiently for her to stop.

"Thanks, Zora, for reaching out to me about Maxim."

"You're welcome," she purred.

He returned his focus to me. "So what sort of trouble have you gotten yourself into now?" He didn't sound angry, just sad.

I stood and gripped the bars. "I'm sorry for disappointing you."

His boots scraped against the cement covered dirt and he stood before me. "Maxim, I'm not disappointed, just heartbroken that you'd give up your gift to be human."

I dropped my head. "Dad, this isn't a gift, it's a curse."

"Maxim, your gift is not a curse. Do you not realize what you are capable of?"

I shook my head. "No."

He nodded. "Well, you were always headstrong. Sit, this story will take a while to tell you." He sighed. "I'm very sorry you are finding out this way instead of when you would've been inducted as the new alpha."

I sat as instructed and waited patiently. Saul sat beside me, and a bowl of popcorn appeared in his lap. "How?" I whispered. "The house's magic doesn't go outside of the house."

He shrugged. "No idea, but let's enjoy it."

"The beginning of the story you know." He glanced at Saul stuffing his face with popcorn. "But I'll go ahead and tell your friend here the story. Centuries ago, when the land was inhabited by the Native Americans, a young son of the chiefs, my grandfather and grandmother, wanted more for their people." He smiled at me. "He was much like you, sort of runs in the genes. Anyway, he had witnessed a young Spanish girl getting kidnapped by his tribe. After, he went to his father and asked him to let her go."

I glanced over at Saul, who had stopped eating popcorn and was enthralled with my dad's story.

My dad smiled and continued. "He vowed to help her, and in doing so changed our tribe forever."

Saul interrupted him, his mouth full of popcorn. "What happened to her?"

My dad just eyed him and continued. "As I was saying, the chief's son wanted more for his tribe. His father was aging and the son would soon be taking over. Soon he fell in love with the Spanish girl, who returned the sentiment. After the father died they banded together to create a tribe that would protect those that were less fortunate. They pulled out all the stops, asking Mother Earth for help in their destiny." He stopped. "This next part, Maxim, is the part not everyone knows. Their answer was in the form of a change in appearance. The elders of the tribe were angry at what he'd done and banished the both of them to their own devices. A few other members followed them, and they were also given the gift of change. From that, they created the Lacomb werewolf pack."

I gasped loudly, and Saul smacked me. "Shh, it's getting interesting."

"So, is that why we're cursed?" I asked.

"It has never been a curse, but a gift, given to us by the most powerful entity. Our powers are brought to life by the very air we breathe, the very ground we walk on. And as alpha of the pack, I'm given special powers to protect my pack and others."

"What kind of powers?" I asked.

"Once you become alpha, you are bestowed with the power of immortality."

I didn't know what to think. "Dad, how come you never told me this?"

He smiled. "I begged you to reconsider your decision to leave. You would have found this out at your ceremony."

I sighed deeply. "I'm sorry, Dad."

"I know. Now let's get you out of here."

"How are you going to do that?" I wondered aloud.

He waved his hand over the lock and it clicked open. "Come now, you need to give up this silly notion of becoming human."

I crossed my arms over my chest. "I can't, Dad. I have to save Mari."

"Who?" he asked with curiosity.

Saul munched on more popcorn. "Oh, that's the fairy your son has fallen in love with." He dropped his popcorn. "Shit, I need to leave. They're starting the competition soon."

My dad turned and stared at the gnome, who shrugged his shoulders.

Saul turned to me. "Stay hidden, friend, until after the competition. I'll protect Mari. I promise. When it's over I'll return." He shifted his hat over his head and stretched out his arms, his shiny rings glistening under the dim light. Zora padded closer to him and wrapped around his legs.

"Zora, how could you allow him to fall in love with a fairy?" Dad asked the cat.

"Sir, Maxim is headstrong. There really was no way of stopping him."

"Very true, but...," he turned to me, "you can't follow through with your feelings."

I grew angry. "Why the hell not?" I demanded.

"Because the both of you come from different worlds." He paused. "Does King Roi know of your feelings?"

I didn't bother asking him about his knowledge of the king since I'd been informed of everyone's knowledge of us. Instead, I nodded. "Yes." A wave of sadness overwhelmed me, but I didn't dare tell him of the deal I'd made with the king. I sat slumped against the wall of my cell and waited patiently for Saul to return. I stood after a few minutes and began pacing back and forth. "What's taking him so long?" I wondered aloud.

"Please, Maxim, calm down." Zora tried to comfort me as I sat waiting for Saul to return.

Suddenly, the walls of the mausoleum shook. Bits of marble fell to the floor as the shaking and rumbling continued. "What the hell is happening?"

"Damn, we need to get Maxim out of here before it crumbles around him." My father's panic was evident in the tone of his voice. The cell door fell, causing a barricade between my father and me. As he tried in vain to move the steel door, parts of the ceiling crashed around me.

Saul ran in, followed by Baron, who immediately lifted the cell door and leaned it against the wall and released me. I crawled out through all the rubble, and couldn't believe what I saw as we safely made our way out.

Twenty-Four

When we stumbled outside of the mausoleum, the cemetery lay in ruins. "What the hell happened?" I asked the loa of the dead.

"Griff has gotten out of hand." His anger resonated in his voice.

I eyed him. "Ya think?"

He seemed angered at my disrespect, but quickly changed when he saw my father standing beside me.

"What happened?" my father asked.

"Mari won the master of domain competition," Saul informed him.

My dad stepped forward placing his hand on my shoulder. "This is what your powers were created for. To help others. It seems as if the fairy may need your help."

Baron tipped his hat and bowed. "Hello, Mr. Rafferty, nice to see you here. To what do I owe a visit from the elite chief of the Lacomb werewolf pack?"

"I've come to regain my son's life."

He eyed my dad. "You do know that if something happens to you, your—"

My father shook his head, interrupting him. "I want my son back."

Baron remained quiet for a few seconds. "On one condition...that he takes care of the damn dragon."

Before he or I could answer, a blast of fire streamed right past us. Saul and I glanced at each other. "We need to stop this now or Griff will burn the entire city down."

The four of us headed to the house, dodging pieces of marble tombs and tree branches. Baron stood off in the distance and looked over his realm. I wondered why he wouldn't just end Griff himself.

"Because I think he wants to see what powers you actually have. The loa of the dead gives you free will to save yourself," my father said from behind me.

As the realm of the dead continued to crash around us, I hurried to the house. Peeking in the window, I saw Mari sitting on a beautiful throne, her blonde hair cascading down and around her shoulders. Even now with all that had happened, she was still beautiful.

Behind me, the crashing and thundering continued. Quickly I walked around the side of the house to the door, which creaked as it opened. Her head popped up and looked in my direction. A smile creased her face briefly.

"Mari...." I stopped, not knowing what to say.

She cocked her head at me. For a second she looked as if she remembered me, but it faded quickly.

"I thought you didn't want this."

"Want what? I don't even know what I am anymore," she said angrily.

"I can help you with that. We just need to get you back home."

She stood from her pearlesque throne, which reminded me so much of the wings that no longer graced her back. She glided down the steps, but when she reached me, she looked straight through me. A thought came to me, and I hoped it would help a little. I removed the amulet from around my neck and looked at her. "Here, Mari, this belongs to you."

Before she could back away from me I reached around and unclipped the necklace that dangled around my neck. I clasped it back around hers. I placed it around. My fingertips grazed her skin and it caused me to shiver. Her softness made me want to pull her closer and feel her lips on mine. Before I could act on my intentions a loud ruckus caused me to run to the door. It flung open and destruction continued outside. In a hurry, I dashed outside into the chaos. My dad and Saul were already knee deep in the shit storm.

As I ran, an invisible force pulled me backward. "What the fuck?" I screamed as it dragged me deep into the ground. I lay on my back in the darkness. It tugged on my legs, and then bit into my leg. Without hesitation I began to shift. My bones cracked, and my body transformed into my second nature. My eyes focused on the dark, and soon I saw what had dragged me into the earth. The creature was nothing like I'd ever seen before. It looked shocked when it realized I could see it. "How?" I asked in a guttural voice.

"No idea...."

It didn't let me finish my sentence as it lunged at me. "You're not supposed to see me until your last breath."

"What are you?" I asked, holding it away from me with one hand.

It stepped back. "I'm a ghoul. My job is to eat the dead. And you, my friend, are standing in my home."

"Does the loa of the dead know you're here?" I asked.

His laugh chilled me to the bone. "Who do you think gave me my home here? I was the one who you couldn't see in the orb competition."

I gasped. "That was you?"

"Yes, now shut up so I can eat you."

I shook my head. "Not going to happen today," I growled.

As he ran at me, I gripped his bony, slimy throat and crunched until his neck oozed in my paws. After wiping off my hands, I crawled back from deep within the earth to see even more destruction. Griff had emblazoned the cemetery. Fire burned bright, but it wasn't moving to the house, so the house was protecting itself. Thank goodness Mari was safely inside it.

As the thought entered my mind, she stepped outside. "No!" I screamed. But my voice was muffled by the blazes around us. When I turned my attention from her, I looked for Griff. There was no sign of him...until off in the distance I saw him. He stood at least ten feet high in his dragon form. His red scales glistened in the light of the moon. To my left, Saul tried to put out a few of the flames, to no avail. My father battled it out with a zombie. I ran over to him, but before I reached him, I was thrown backward. When I looked up I stared into the face of Griff...well, his dragon face.

"Why are you doing this?"

"Because I was supposed to win." He sneered at me. "Somehow, Saul helped Mari win."

My laugh boomed loudly. "Is that so? I thought you wanted her for your...uh...little plan."

He grabbed me by the throat, his wings flapping around behind him. His claws dug into my neck, drawing blood that dripped down my black fur. I dangled like a rag doll, but I willed myself to stay alive. From the corner of my eye, I saw my father running on all fours, heading in my direction. I howled loudly, then dug my teeth into the hard scales on Griff's arm.

"Fuck!" he shouted and dropped me. When I glanced back at my father, it was too late. As soon as he got inches from me a huge fireball slammed into his body. In a matter of seconds, he fell to the ground, burning.

"No!" I screamed in agony, turning and facing Griff. "You'll pay for this." I ran toward him, pulling out the gift from Cassandra. When I pushed the button on the knife the blade clicked open. Glancing at the inscription, I read....

Quod incepimus conficiemus
"What we have begun we shall finish."

I read the inscription without any hesitation. As I did, the blade glowed a light blue as the sword emerged. It slid effortlessly from the small handle, magically becoming a heavy sword. The blade showed Griff's maniacal reflection. He shied away from it for a second. From my peripheral vision, I saw Baron Samedi flushing the fire away from my father's body. I knew he'd be all right since he was immortal, though my anger erupted full force at the dragon. I held my sword tightly and lunged at him, raising the sword high, but just as I swung it Mari stepped between us.

"Please, Maxim." She reached out and touched my arm, causing my heart to break. Sadness crept slowly over my face. "You're right, I didn't want this. I need to go with him. I must protect the fairies."

"You remember?" I dropped the blade, letting the point dig into the soft dirt, and sighed.

"Some, with the help of Eloise."

I gently touched the amulet that I'd returned to her. It warmed as I held it. "This should help a little more. Don't do this. I can help you. It's my destiny." Regret played havoc with my thoughts as I turned back to see the body of my father sprawled on the ground. Baron stood over him with a grim expression on his face.

With her fingertips, she turned my face back to hers, and the touch sent tingles through my body. When I faced her again, she kissed me. The taste of her tears lingered as she spoke against my lips. "I've never felt anything like the feelings I have for you."

As the world stopped around me, I leaned into Mari, letting my senses take in all of her. Her scent, of magnolias and the sun, tickled my nose as if she had waved the white flower petals in my direction. I brushed a hand along her arm, relishing in the softness of her skin. "Say my name," I pleaded with her.

She obliged me. "Max," she breathed out, and I forever imprinted it in my memories.

"Mari, you are the most beautiful creature I have ever laid eyes on." I traced the edges of her face and stared at her, vowing never to forget the soft lines, the way her nose turned upward, and the way she still blushed at my touch. When she kissed me one last time, I swore never to forget the sweetness of her lips on mine. She stood to leave me and whispered, "I will forever love you."

Griff stood a few feet back with a smug grin on his face. Mari solemnly walked toward him and grabbed his hand. They walked off, leaving me to deal with the loneliness that wrapped around me.

Twenty-Five

As Mari and Griff disappeared through the trees guarding the cemetery, I couldn't help but want to scream. Then I remember my father. I crawled to him. Baron Samedi knelt beside him.

"I'm sorry, Maxim, he doesn't have much time left."

"Wait...no...what...?" I stammered. "He's an alpha...he's immortal."

My dad tried to speak but only coughed.

"Don't try to speak," Baron told my dad.

"He'll get better," I said as I gripped his hand, his skin peeling back from the bones.

"No, he won't."

I looked up, trying not to let the loa see me cry.

Saul's hand patted my shoulder. "I'm so sorry, Max."

I shook my head. "No, he's immortal, he can't be dying."

"I'm afraid he is." Before I could interrupt him, he continued. "You see, even though the house is protected by magic, the cemetery is all mine. And his immortality was forfeited when he stepped into my land." He waved his hands. "This is the underworld."

A wave of anger erupted throughout me. "You'll reverse this." I went to stand, but my father's hand gently tugged on me.

"Maxim," he choked out, his voice barely recognizable. "I need you to go home and become alpha of our pack."

I shook my head. "No, you will be better in no time."

He patted my hand. "Son, it's your time. I've lived long enough. I've seen the world, but most importantly, I've loved. Bring me back home and give me a proper burial."

Tears slid down my face, but underneath my sadness, my hatred for Griff grew. "Dad," I sobbed, dropping my head, hiding my sadness.

"Maxim, don't hide your emotions. They are what makes us great alphas." He turned to the loa. "Can you do something about this horrible pain?"

"Yes, it will pass soon." He waved his hand over my father.

"Before I go, son, know that I'm extremely proud of you. One other thing. If you truly love the fairy, you must save her and the others."

I wiped away a tear and nodded my head. "I will." I didn't dare tell him that I owed the king a debt and feared how I would tell him I'd lost Mari. He would rescind his pride in me. I held my dad's hand as he drifted away. I watched his heart beat one last time, leaving his chest silent and unmoving.

I stood and spoke. "Baron Samedi, would you do me a favor?"

He bowed. "For the future alpha of the Lacomb pack? Anything within reason. You must give me an offering."

Saul tapped me on the thigh. I looked at the gnome, who held a few items.

"How did you know? Better yet, where did you get these?"

"I figured you would be asking him for a favor when your father died. When I planned on coming into the house I figured they would come in handy."

He handed me the items.

I turned and faced the loa and handed him the items. He eyed the bottle of rum and the box of cigars. He smiled. "These will do just fine. Now, what may I do for you?"

"Can you wrap the body for transport back home?" I asked, choking back my sadness.

He nodded. Within seconds, my dad's body was wrapped tightly in a muslin fabric.

"Thanks, Baron Samedi."

"You are welcome. I have a favor to ask of you. Could you please recapture Griff and bring him to me?"

A grin spread across my face. "It would be my pleasure."

I glanced at the body of the one person I vowed to never disappoint again. Now I needed to get back home and tell my mom.

Baron patted me on the back. "Maxim, I'll take care of sending his body back to your family."

"I need to get there before he does to warn Mom."

He shook his head. "I've already sent Zora to warn them."

Saul stood beside me, and I turned back to the loa. "Can Saul's life be spared?"

He pondered this for a second. "Sure, the outcome of this has gone beyond my expectations. Besides, I've gotten two deaths. I'll call that a win for my side." He grinned wide.

"Thank you." I nudged Saul. "How do you feel about joining me on my mission of bringing Griff back here?"

He removed his hat and scratched his black hair. Quickly he replaced it and looked up at me. "Why the hell not? After all, I could use an adventure."

"Good, let's get going. I've got to take my rightful place as alpha and capture Griff." We walked off past the huge cypress trees and headed home. "You know, Saul, I think this is the beginning of—"

He stopped me. "Don't get all mushy on me." He tried to hide a huge smile. "We will be friends forever."

Epilogue

I stared in silence at the body of my father. Never in a million years had I ever expected him to be gone. The slight touch of my mother's hand on my back brought me back to the now. "He was, and will be forever, proud of you."

"I know, Mom, but I failed him." My shoulders slumped.

"That is impossible. No matter what you've done in the past," she reassured me. "Now we need to prepare his body for cremation and spread him across the earth, where his powers will be sent back to where they came from."

I reached an arm out and draped it over her. "Mom, I'm so sorry this happened."

She sniffed and I glanced at her. She wiped the tears away. "Don't be. He knew the consequences of going to the underworld.

Something you must remember when you have gained your immortality."

I nodded. "I will."

"Good." She smiled kindly. "Now go take care of your gnome friend before he's banished from here. He's driving everyone crazy. Besides, you need to get ready for the ceremony."

I hugged her tight and gazed into the dark eyes. It was always said I got my Spanish looks from my father, but I'd gotten my kindness from her. "I love you, Mom."

"Love you too, son."

A few hours later

The moon shone brightly in the sky as we assembled outside. The pine trees flanked around us. My mother stood to my right, holding my father's ashes in a pottery urn. Her hands shook as she held it tightly. A couple emerged from behind the circle. Their familiarity caused me to gasp, though they looked as if they hadn't aged in decades.

I leaned in closer and whispered to Mom, "Is that...?"

She grinned. "Yes, the creators of our pack. They only come back when a new alpha is named."

The couple walked forward. The man spoke first. "Hello, Maxim, so nice to see you all grown.

I think the last time was when you were just a pup. We just wish your father was here to join us."

Both resembled my father and me. I blinked a couple of times, not wanting to believe they were still alive. But then, I remembered they were immortal. "How...why...?" I stammered.

They both laughed. "We understand what you are trying to ask. We had to leave when a new alpha took his rightful place. Since we are the creators, there would be too much power to allow the new alpha to take charge."

"Wait...do you mean my mom and dad would have left?"

"Yes, I'm afraid so. Now your mother will be coming with us. Like us and the others after us, our energy will remain to help you during your first year. You must learn how to lead by yourself after that."

A wave of sadness crept through my bones. My mother leaned into me. "Don't worry, you will make a fine alpha."

"Let the ceremony begin. First, we will spread Eustache's ashes into the earth so that his powers will be returned to where they belong." He turned to the crowd. "As you know, with all the alphas of your pack, each time a new alpha is named we lose a bit of our magic. But we share it with the new alpha." He took the urn from my mother and knelt on the ground, opened it, and spread the contents along the ground. The ashes seeped into the earth as if they were being called back home. Once it was done, he stood. Then he turned to me. "Sit, Maxim."

I did as he instructed. As my body touched the ground, he started to chant and dance around me. He prayed to Mother Earth to bestow on me the greatest of all powers. The earth began to shake and answer him. All of a sudden I was thrown to the ground and a strong power infused all around me. A burning sensation erupted throughout my body. The sky opened pouring its tears down around me. My bones cracked and I started to shift, but just as I did, I returned to my human self. This continued for so long I lost track of time. Finally, I slumped to the ground, exhausted, with my wet hair plastered to me. I sighed deeply.

"It's over, son. Now you must choose a wife."

My head jerked in surprise. Holy shit, they weren't going to like my choice.

I choked out. "I choose Mariwen, fairy of the feu follet fairies." Gasps from all my pack echoed around me on the air. I smiled. "I'm sorry, Mom, but I have a debt I need to repay to the loa of the dead, and a fairy to save."

She smiled at me. "Then go, son."

"Are you sure? What about the pack?"

"I can handle that until you repay your debt. Besides, the wife of the alpha must be strong in her own right. Now go and save your fairy."

The end, or is it...

LISTS OF BOOKS

Voodoo Vows
Magical Memories
Voodoo Vows Book 1
Ghosts from the Past Book
Black Magic Betrayal Book 2
Spellbound Sacrifice Book 3
Ghosts from the Present

The Guardians a Voodoo Vows Tail
Bred by Magic Book 1
Gifted by Magic Book 2

The Cresent City Sentries
Stone Hearts

Bayou Kiss Series
Summer's Kiss

A Legacy Falls Novella
An Unexpected Hero

Brotherhood of Redemption
The Protector's Kiss

Coming Soon
Devine Descent
Trapped by Magic
Stone Player
Autum's Kiss
The Gryphon's Revenge
The Bear's Redemption

About the Author

As a young girl, Diana Marie Dubois was an avid reader and was often found in the local public library. Now you find her working in her local library. Hailing from the culture filled state of Louisiana, just outside of New Orleans; her biggest inspiration has always been the infamous Anne Rice and her tales of Vampires. It was those very stories that inspired Diana to take hold of her dreams and begin writing. She lives in the country with her Great Dane Elysia.

Facebook:
https://www.facebook.com/diana.m.dubois

Goodreads
https://www.goodreads.com/author/show/769066
2.Diana_Marie_DuBois

Instagram:
http://instagram.com/dianamariedubois

Pintererst:
http://www.pinterest.com/dianamdubois/

Twitter: https://twitter.com/DianaMDuBois

Tumblr: http://dianamariedubois.tumblr.com/

Website: www.dianamariedubois.com